T0193106

THE CHRONICLES
OF EBONI STEELE

HOPE AMBER REIGN

authorHOUSE®

AuthorHouse™
1663 Liberty Drive
Bloomington, IN 47403
www.authorhouse.com
Phone: 1 (800) 839-8640

Published by AuthorHouse 06/02/2020

ISBN: 978-1-7283-0479-3 (sc)
ISBN: 978-1-7283-0477-9 (hc)
ISBN: 978-1-7283-0478-6 (e)

Library of Congress Control Number: 2019903279

Print information available on the last page.

This book is dedicated to:

every fatherless daughter and woman who never experienced love from her father. I hope you will be uplifted and inspired to live your life to the fullest. You are worthy to be loved and deserve to live a wonderful life. Release your pain and seek healing for your soul. Live out your wildest dreams and believe you can do anything you set your mind out to do. Remember to love yourself first and always have faith in God.

Love, Hope Amber Reign

INTRODUCTION

The Chronicles of Eboni Steele is a narrative about Eboni, who is African American and a fatherless girl. Her story is a journal that chronicles her life from birth to 34 years old.

Raised in the suburbs of Lincoln City, Maryland, in the '70s, she struggled with her identity throughout her life. She felt like an outcast because of the color of her skin. Eboni craved attention and acceptance from her peers.

Every Sunday, she attended church with her grandmother, Mamma G. When she was 13 years old, she converted to the Mormon faith.

At age 18, she met her father Mel. Eboni hoped her father wanted a father-daughter relationship with her. As a result of not having a loving relationship with him, Eboni looked for love in all the wrong places. She reflected on her failed relationships with men, and yearned to feel loved by a man. Seeking validation from every man she dated, she realized the importance of practicing self-love.

She matured into a beautiful black woman who finally embraced her self-worth. Eboni renewed her faith in God, taking ownership for her mistakes, her life experiences and the choices she made. She restored her faith in God, forgave her father and released herself from the pain of being a fatherless daughter.

1
MY FAMILY

MEET MY GRANDMOTHER MAMMA G

Eugenia Lynn Lee, aka Mamma G, was the rock of the family. She was born on April 10, 1910 in Bennington, South Carolina to her parents, Tina and Fred Lee. My great grandmother, Tina Lee, died from malaria, when Mamma G was two years old. Malaria was a disease that plagued the South in the early 1900s. When Tina died, my great grandfather, Fred Lee, solicited support from his village of family members and close friends to help raise his daughter, Mamma G.

Mamma G had six children with my grandfather, William, but their marriage didn't last long. Unable to resolve issues in their relationship, my grandmother and grandfather decided to end their union and went their separate ways. When she was 46 years old, Mamma G migrated north to Maryland to find employment and a home for her and her children.

Mamma G, the epitome of class and style, was my hero. She was petite and stood at only 5 feet tall. She had beautiful and distinct facial features, her silky skin and light complexion, long pointy nose, and small eyes emphasized her beauty. Her coal black hair was always well-groomed with small and tight pressed curls. She wore bright pink lipstick to accentuate her small thin lips. The moles on the right side of her face and above her cheeks were her beauty marks.

Mamma G was a praying woman with grace and style. She was also very meticulous. Every morning, she used a can of starch to iron her clothes, sheets, and pillowcases for a neat, crisp finish. Whenever she ran an errand or went to the store, she wore her white satin gloves. She spent her entire life as a domestic worker who cooked and cleaned houses of affluent families in Lincoln City.

Acting as a surrogate mom, she spent over 10 hours a day in their homes. Mamma G raised her employers' children from birth until they graduated from high school. The well-to-do attorneys, doctors, and nurses who employed her; made her feel like a member of their family. She was always captured in family photos. They invited her to family gatherings, birthdays, and holiday festivities.

MEET MY MOM FRAN

My mother, Fran Louise Lee, was born in the small town of Bennington, South Carolina on June 6, 1940 to Eugenia Lynn and William Lee. The fifth of six children, she had two brothers and three sisters. African Americans faced many hardships because of the racial inequities of living in the South. The repercussions of slavery and Jim Crow laws made it difficult for people of color to become viable members of their communities.

William and Eugenia did what they could to keep food on the table and a roof over the heads for their family of eight. Grandpa William, a sharecropper and the breadwinner of the family, could barely provide the basics for his children. The discriminatory and illegal practices of white landowners made it difficult for him to prosper.

Ultimately, the financial strain led to the dissolution of his marriage to my grandmother. They split up their children and sent them to live with different family members. Mamma G moved to Maryland, and William went to New York. Their separation impacted the family and children for the rest of their lives.

My mom lived with Aunt Lynn, Mamma G's older sister, after her parents separated. Aunt Lynn raised my mom as if she were her own daughter. After a while, living in a small town wasn't where she wanted to reside. She missed her mother and wanted to begin a new chapter in her life. Mamma G told her she could live with her in Lincoln City, Maryland.

During the summer of 1957, at the age of 17, my mother left Bennington and moved to Lincoln City, to live with her mother Mamma G. Lincoln City was nothing like Bennington. There were so many people walking about and hanging out on street corners almost 24 hours a day. Living in a metropolis was different than residing in a small southern town because there were so many things to do and people to meet.

The first few weeks after her move from Bennington to Lincoln City were hard for my mom. She missed Mamma G's older brother, her uncle, Fred Eades. He was her favorite relative. When she lived in Bennington, at the end of each school day, she walked down a long narrow road to visit his diner. Mamma G's older brother, Fred Eades, and a group of sharecroppers built the diner with their bare hands in the summer of 1930. The brown shack-like building was located in the backwoods of town.

During that time, blacks were banned from white restaurants and establishments. The diner was a gathering place for African American sharecroppers and members of their community. On Friday nights, the people of Bennington congregated to socialize, listen to music playing from the jukebox, dance, and enjoy Southern cuisine. It was their special place to escape the adversities and perpetual racial inequities of living in the South.

Uncle Fred anticipated Fran's arrival to the diner like clockwork. He'd greet her at the front door and say, "Welcome to my cafe!" The aroma of fried chicken made Fran's mouth water. Knowing she was hungry, Uncle Fred would ask her, "Would you like something to eat?"

Delighted, Fran immediately answered, "Yes." Ten minutes later, Uncle Fred strolled out of the kitchen with a brown paper bag. Inside was a fried chicken sandwich, a red apple, and pop to take home. As she left Uncle Fred's diner, Fran waved goodbye with a big grin on her face. She'd always say, "Thank you, Uncle Fred. I'll see you tomorrow."

As Fran reminisced about life in Bennington and her past encounters with Uncle Fred, she smiled. After a few weeks of living in Lincoln City, Fran began to settle into her new home. Mesmerized by the sights, sounds, skyscrapers, and overcrowded streets, Fran grew accustomed to the city life. Bennington, with its population of about 500 people, was the complete opposite of her new home in Lincoln City, which had 5,000 people.

By the fall, Fran had started her senior year at Lincoln High School. She made some friends within the first few days because they were intrigued by her accent. Every day someone asked her where she was from. Proudly, emphasizing her Southern drawl, Fran responded, "Bennington, South Carolina."

One day, Fran strutted into the school cafeteria and caught the attention of one of the star basketball players, Charles Davis. She loved to show off her cute, curvy-shaped body, caramel complexion, and thick long hair. Wearing a cute afro, clad in a red and white striped jumpsuit and platform shoes, she was the latest attraction. Her new classmates waited for her at the long white table in the lunchroom. The boys and the girls eyeballed one another. While eating their lunch, the girls congregated and conversed about the boys they admired.

During 4th period, Charles saw Fran walking down the crowded hallway and followed her. "Hey. What's your name? Can I walk with you?" Charles spoke with a deep voice that seemed a little shaky. Fran remembered seeing him in the cafeteria.

Although she usually dressed to impress and acted like she was always confident, Fran was a shy introvert. She didn't know what to say to Charles, so she quietly whispered, "My name is Fran. What's your name?" Immediately, Charles began to grin. He proudly uttered, "My name is Charles."

Without missing a beat, as if they were both thinking the same thing, the two began to stroll down the corridor to Fran's next class. Once they reached the door, Fran waved goodbye to him and walked into her English class. She couldn't stay focused on her school-work because she kept thinking about what happened in the hallway when she met Charles.

Charles was a point guard and superstar player on Lincoln's basketball team. Standing at 6 feet and 4 inches tall, he towered over his other teammates. At the last home game against their rivals, the Lexington Rams, Charles scored over 30 points. His athletic build and good looks captivated all the girls. Fran felt intimidated because he was so popular. Ashamed of her Southern drawl, she doubted he would ever really be interested in her. She wasn't like the other girls.

Once the school day ended, Fran started on her walk home. As she left the building, she heard footsteps getting closer to her. She turned around to see Charles making his way toward her. When they finally stood face to face, she blushed. She was enamored by his smile and physical presence. Charles finally broke the silence. "Do you mind if I tag along?" He offered to walk her home.

Fran gave him a smile of approval. Even though she was unsure why Charles was paying her so much attention, she wanted to get to know him. Fran inquired about his family life. He told her he lived with his mother and grandmother. They continued talking until they ended up at the front door of Fran's apartment building.

Before she walked up the steps, Charles asked Fran for a piece of paper. "Write down your phone number. I'll call you when I finish my homework." Fran couldn't believe that he asked for her number and wanted to call her. She tore a piece of paper out of her notebook and gave it to him.

Over the next couple of weeks, Charles waited by Fran's locker to greet her every day. On Valentine's Day, he surprised her with a special gift. As she walked towards him, he hid her gift behind his back. "Close your eyes." Excited to see her reaction, he said, "Now open them! Happy Valentine's Day!"

Charles gave her a bouquet of roses and a small white jewelry box. Elated, she took the flowers and box from him and thanked him. Removing the red ribbon, she couldn't wait to see what was inside. Inside the box was a shiny, beautiful gold ring. Fran didn't know if the ring was real gold or not, but she didn't care. Pulling Charles close to her, she pecked him on the cheek. Strutting to class, Fran smiled from ear-to-ear as she proudly toted her gifts.

She craved love and attention, the things she never felt from her dad. After her parents separated, her life was never the same. The void left by her father's separation from her mom caused Fran to leave her heart open and exposed. Because she often felt unloved, she was vulnerable and naive when it came to her relationships with men.

Although she barely knew Charles, she instantly fell for him. Dating him made her feel special. Within three months, they were a couple and saying those three little words to each other. Fran believed he was the love of her life. She had never been told she was loved by a man until she met Charles.

As the school year continued, Fran and Charles were inseparable. You didn't see one without the other. Charles loved her calming spirit and charming personality. In mid-April, they attended prom as a couple. The night of the gala, over 100 seniors and their dates packed the school's cafeteria.

The cafeteria was decorated with balloons and red and white streamers. Charles wore a black tuxedo with a red dress shirt and a white bow tie. He was as sharp as a tack. Instead of his usual cornrows, he wore his hair in an afro that was tamed and picked. Fran looked like a beautiful black African queen. She wore a long baby blue gown with short ruffled sleeves. Her hair was pulled back in a bun.

At the end of the night, Charles drove Fran to his apartment. His mother and grandmother were already asleep. They snuck into his bedroom and made out until 2:00 in the morning. Fran ignored her mother's orders to be home by curfew. Charles was Fran's first love, so they wanted their prom night to be special without any time limits. They wanted to be intimate.

Taking a breath between kisses, Fran looked at the clock. Realizing it was almost morning, she feared Mamma G would kick her out of the house. Fran panicked and insisted that Charles take her home. "Hurry! I want to get in before she wakes up." Charles drove quickly to Fran's house and watched her sneak into Mamma G's home.

Fran and Charles continued dating after graduating from high school. Two months later, they were expecting a baby. Mamma G was disappointed that Fran had gotten pregnant out of wedlock. She was concerned about how the church members would respond to the news. Mamma G insisted Fran and Charles get married.

Initially, Charles was against the idea of marriage. He didn't see the value or purpose of making that kind of commitment. His father never married his mother. Charles grew up without a father in his home. He thought getting married was pointless. Eventually, Fran convinced him that marriage was the right thing to do. "Don't you want your child to grow up with a father in the home? We can start our new life together like a family." She made her case and won Charles over. Plus, he wanted to prove he loved her.

In the summer of 1958, Fran and Charles united as one in holy matrimony. It was a beautiful day in August. Mamma G, her friend, Ms. Ruth, Charles' mother, as well as his grandmother witnessed their small ceremony at the justice of the peace. No other family members or friends were invited to the private ceremony. Fran wanted to make her mom happy by protecting Mamma G's reputation at church.

On her wedding day, Fran wore an off-white dress that hid her baby bump. Charles wore a black suit with a white dress shirt and tie. Their wedding ceremony lasted 20 minutes. Afterwards, they went to Mamma

G's house to celebrate their nuptials. She served fried chicken, macaroni and cheese, greens, and her famous pound cake.

The next day, Fran and Charles moved into a spacious one-bedroom basement apartment on Fountain Street. It was two blocks from his mother and grandmother's house. To support his family, Charles worked full-time at the local grocery store. It wasn't the greatest job, but he knew he had to do something to support his family. Charles contemplated joining the military instead of going to college. Once the baby was born, he thought he would enlist in the Army.

Charles hated his job because he didn't like one of the managers. Every night, he complained about how he treated him. He claimed his manager, Thomas, constantly picked on him. Every day, Charles threatened to quit his job. Fran begged him to not leave until he found another one. They needed his income to pay rent and take care of the baby. Fran began to suspect that her husband's discontentment would lead to him losing his job, so, she began to stash a few dollars away.

Fran's suspicions were right. A few weeks before the baby was due, Charles came home and told her he had gotten fired from his job. She couldn't believe it. The baby was due in a few weeks and they needed Charles' paycheck. Without his income, Fran knew she had to get a job almost immediately after the baby was born.

Not knowing what to do, Fran called her mom and asked for help finding work. Mamma G cleaned the house of a popular lawyer in town, Mr. Lawrence, so she asked him to give Fran a job after she had the baby. He took a gamble on her because he knew Mamma G was a hard worker and trusted her judgement. Mr. Lawrence told Mamma G that he had a law clerk position available and would hold the job open for Fran. After she had the baby, she could begin working at his law firm downtown.

Tragically, at 36 years old, Charles' mother, Mary Davis, died. His grandmother called Fran to give her and Charles the bad news. Every day since she was diagnosed with diabetes, Charles took care of his mom. She succumbed to the disease two weeks before the baby was due.

Charles had a loving relationship with his mother. They had a strong bond. Everyone called him a "mama's boy" because of it. Mary had him at 17 years old, right after she graduated from high school. Mary raised Charles as a single mom. He was her first and only child. She was his number one fan. From the time he was a little boy, she never missed a school assembly, an award ceremony or basketball games.

Mourning Mary's sudden death, Charles stayed in the house for two weeks. He'd lie in bed day in and day out. Depression began to set in. Fran began to notice empty liquor bottles on the side of their bed. She realized Charles had been drinking. Every day, he stayed to himself in their bedroom for hours.

After his mother passed, he changed. Each day, he seemed agitated over little things. Days went by without them talking to each other. His drinking increased. The more he drank, the more he lashed out at her. Pregnant and concerned about the wellbeing of her baby, Fran feared for her life.

One Friday afternoon, she was at home alone. Fran went into labor. She endured 10 hours of contractions and pain because Charles hadn't come home. With the help from one of her girlfriends, she made it to the hospital in time to deliver her baby. The doctor proudly announced the baby was a boy.

On May 13, 1959, Calvin was born at Lincoln City Regional Hospital. He weighed 7 pounds and 6 ounces. After the nurse checked his vitals, she rolled him to Fran's room. Charles was anxiously waiting to see his son. When the nurse opened the door with Calvin in her arms, he reached out for his son.

Lovingly, Charles welcomed his son. "Hello Calvin. Daddy couldn't wait to see you." Mamma G was across town cleaning a house, so she missed the birth of her grandson. She got to the hospital as soon as she could. It was a joyous day for the young couple. Charles smiled for the first since his mother passed.

Calvin brought a lot of happiness to their family. He started crawling at six months and was walking by the time he was 10 months old. Fran and Charles could barely keep up with him. His antics seemed to bring light into their unhappy marriage. However, Charles' unpredictable mood swings and temper were concerning at times. Fran never knew when he would become enraged. Him being unemployed made matters worse. Fran prayed he would stop drinking and find a new job.

The day Charles lashed out at Calvin was the last straw. Fran could tell he was intoxicated and agitated when he came in from the grocery store. Annoyed at Calvin for spilling milk on the living room floor Charles yelled, "What the hell is wrong with you?" Running out of the room, Fran screamed, "He's just a baby. Stop shouting at him!"

Charles grabbed Calvin by his shirt collar, causing Calvin to cry out for Fran. Instantly, Fran rushed to her son's side and wiped away the tears running down his little cheeks. Once she had calmed Calvin down, Fran approached Charles so she could understand why he was so upset. Without any warning, Charles raised his hand and slapped her in the face.

"Shut the f*** up!" Charles was in no mood to take any lip from her.

As Fran hit the floor, Calvin ran to latch on to her leg and began sobbing uncontrollably. Charles couldn't take the hysterics anymore. He grabbed his coat and stormed out of the house.

Holding one hand over her eye in disbelief, Fran cried. She didn't understand why Charles had assaulted her. The person who had stood in front of her minutes ago was not the loving man she had married. Many thoughts rushed through her mind. Should she stay in the marriage or leave?

Fran was a transplant from Bennington, a small town in South Carolina where she had never seen a man abuse his wife. The men in her hometown were loving toward their wives and family members. She didn't want to be another statistic raising a black male without a father, but their safety was more important.

Fran took Calvin into the bedroom and locked the door. Even though she was still hurt, she hoped Charles would come back home so they could talk about what happened. Time away from one another is what she thought they needed to get their marriage back on track. Fran wanted time to heal from his physical and verbal abuse. She hoped he would seek professional help about his drinking and battle with depression.

Planning a temporary getaway, she called her mom for help. Around midnight, Charles finally returned home. The next morning, when Charles left for the day, Fran packed what she could in a couple of suitcases, took her son, and left the apartment to go to Mamma G's. She knew she could always depend on her mom when she needed her.

Fran's plan was to stay at her mom's place for a month until things settled down with Charles. Taking a break from her husband was a temporary fix for their failing marriage. After one week, she wanted to go back home to restore their relationship. She missed living in her own place. If he had apologized and acknowledged what had happened, the relationship could get back on track.

Mamma G agreed to babysit Calvin so that Fran could go back to work. The wages she earned at the law firm only covered diapers and formula. One day, Charles called Fran with news that he couldn't find a job and had changed his mind about enlisting in the Army. He told Fran that the landlord gave him an eviction notice to move out of their basement apartment in 30 days.

It appeared that he was too depressed to care for anything other than drinking all day and night. He told her he didn't care and moved back home with his grandmother. Fran didn't know what she was going to do because it felt like her world was crashing in on her. She had to figure out how she would retrieve the rest of her belongings and break the bad news to Mamma G.

As if she wasn't under enough pressure, Fran didn't have a car. She took public transportation everywhere she went. Now that she had to take Calvin to his routine doctor appointments, she couldn't depend on the bus to arrive on schedule. Some days she waited at the bus stop for up to 20 minutes only to find out it had been delayed for some reason.

Even though Mamma G had offered to help her buy a car, Fran had always been too proud to accept. Realizing that she needed transportation, Fran finally agreed to let her mom help her. Both Mamma G and Fran could benefit from having reliable transportation. Fran could take her to church or to the store when she needed because Mamma G didn't know how to drive.

One Saturday morning, Fran, Mamma G, and Calvin took the F11 bus to a used car dealership. They walked onto the lot and saw a plethora of cars.

A gentleman greeted them. "Hello. Can I help you?"

Excited about buying a car, Fran asked him about the price of the first car she saw that she liked. Once the salesman told her the price, Fran looked at her mom and smiled because it was just the amount they could afford to pay. Fran filled out the paperwork to purchase the used white 1955 4-door Dodge Series. She was so happy to finally have a car instead of having to rely on public transportation.

The used car was a clunker with low mileage and a couple of dents on the trunk. In the backseat of the passenger side, the seat cover was ripped, and it definitely looked like it had been through somethings. Fran didn't care because everything else worked. After signing on the dotted lines to complete her purchase, Fran jumped in the driver seat and drove them back home.

The next day she was excited about driving around town in her new ride. Fran drove to her girlfriend's birthday party. Dressed up in her cute navy-blue jumpsuit and brown platform shoes, she couldn't wait to get to the party to show off her outfit. Her hair was in an afro puff pulled up into a ponytail. On her way to the party, Fran stopped by People's Drug Stop to pick up a birthday card.

While standing in the cashier's line, a man approached her. "Hey pretty lady. You are so fine." Giving her compliments, he hoped she would turn around and acknowledge him. She kept her head facing the cashier and ignored him. He kept talking and even had the nerve to ask Fran if he could take her out on a date.

Fran still loved Charles and hoped to reconcile with him after he got the professional help he needed. Meeting someone new was the last thing she wanted to do. Keeping her family together was her priority. She remained focused on getting to her girlfriend's birthday party on time.

Fran paid the cashier and waved goodbye to her new admirer. He followed her out of the store. "Hey. Can we at least be friends?" He rushed outside still following behind her to help open her car door. Fran smiled at him as she put her key in the ignition. She didn't know what it was about him. Maybe she liked his persistence.

Insisting that she give him a chance by giving him her phone number, the mystery man introduced himself as Mel Jones. Mel was tall, dark-skinned, and cleaned up nicely. He went on and on about how he was a good man and a great catch. Fran didn't know what came over her, but she liked what he was saying and listened to him. She waited patiently for him to end his rant.

Mel told her he was single, owned his own home, and had a great job. Fran couldn't help but wonder if this man was for real. Could he really be such a wonderful man? After she'd heard Mel talk for what seemed like an hour, Fran agreed to give him her number. Mel quickly reached into his jacket pocket to grab a pen, then he wrote Fran's name and number on the back of his receipt. He stood in the parking lot and waved goodbye until her car was out of sight.

Mel didn't waste any time. He called Fran the next day. Determined to win her over, he called to offer to have her car repaired at his job. He said he'd noticed her new car tags and wanted to make sure the vehicle was safe to drive. Surprised that a total stranger would offer to help her in that kind of way, Fran grew suspicious of his motives.

Over the next several days, Mel called Fran to check on her. Their conversations were usually about how he would take care of her. She seemed confused by his wanting to help without knowing her that well. At the end of the week, he called and offered to take Fran out to dinner. She declined and told him she was married and wanted to reconcile with her husband.

Despite learning that Fran was still attached to her husband, Mel continued in his pursuit. He told her he wanted to be friends with no strings attached. "You are a beautiful woman Fran. I can be a good friend." She thought it was too good to be true.

Mel remained consistent and called her twice a week. He was a car salesman and had the gift of gab. Slowly, he began to gain her trust. Every chance he could, he expressed how he would be good to her. Hearing how much he wanted a family made Fran vulnerable. She yearned to have a family and a father for her son.

Over the next few weeks, Fran and Mel talked on the phone every day. She started falling for him. As much as she wanted to save her marriage, Charles seemed like he didn't care either way. He hadn't seen her or Calvin in months. When she called him to discuss their relationship, he would make an excuse about why he hadn't called.

Eventually, Fran looked forward to talking to Mel every day. His sense of humor and charming personality stirred up her feelings. He made her smile. When he didn't call, she was disappointed. Each time they talked, she felt him becoming more than a friend. Even though she expressed to Mel that she remained hopeful that she would reconcile with her husband, he continued in his pursuit.

Even though Fran loved the time and attention she got from Mel, there was something about him that didn't feel quite right. For one thing, he was

10 years older than her. What single and eligible bachelor willingly dated a young single mother? Why was he so fascinated by her? Fran questioned his motives, but not enough to end their friendship.

After weeks of putting up a front like she didn't want to date Mel, Fran eventually fell for his charm and agreed to go out to dinner with him. She didn't tell her mom about him because she feared she would receive unnecessary judgment. Instead, on the night of her date with Mel, Fran told her mom she was going to hang out with a girlfriend.

Fran had a great time at dinner with Mel. The topic of their conversation remained the same. All Mel could talk about was how he wanted to be there for her and Calvin. He even offered to pay for daycare. When he dropped her back at home to Mamma G's house, he handed her $100 in cash.

Earlier in the week, she reached out to Charles to inquire about the status of their relationship, but he wasn't home. It had been over six months, and he hadn't shown any signs of wanting to get back together. If he didn't want to be married, Fran wanted to know. But why didn't he want to spend time with his son? The thought of Calvin not having a father in his life was devastating to her because she grew up without her father in her life.

After months of testing Mel to see if he was for real, Fran finally introduced him to Calvin. She decided he could be a good role model and father figure for him. More than anything, Fran felt Calvin needed to spend time hanging out with a man. The only male in his life was Uncle Van but he lived in New York.

On a beautiful sunny day in April, Mel met them at the playground around the corner from Fran's mother's apartment. He waved to Fran as he walked toward her near the playground. She pointed to Calvin having fun on the sliding board. They walked over to him and Mel introduced himself. Before Mel could strike up a conversation with Calvin, he ran over to the monkey bars to play with his friends. Then Mel followed him and started passing a football to Calvin and his friends.

From that day at the playground, Mel did all kinds of things with Calvin. They tossed a football around and played catch almost every time they were together. Watching Mel interact with her son, Fran began falling for him. He treated Calvin like his own son. They had formed a bond so quickly that Fran thought it was a sign. She thought Mel was the one. The playground became Mel and Calvin's meeting spot.

After dating Mel for over a year, Fran began to consider moving on and ending her marriage with Charles. He never put effort into trying to reconcile or make their marriage work, so she gave up. After going a year without any real communication, she decided to file for a divorce. The attorney who worked in her office told her it could take up to a year for the divorce to be finalized.

After she filed the paperwork to legally end her marriage to Charles, Fran began to rethink her living situation. Staying in her mother's tiny 2-bedroom apartment wasn't where she wanted her and her son to be. Mel had extended an offer for her and Calvin to move into his new home. She declined until her divorce was final because she was still legally married.

Fran never introduced Mel to her mom because she knew Mamma G wouldn't approve. Despite everything that had happened, Fran knew her mom didn't want her to give up on her marriage. She kept reminding her of the wedding vows she made with her husband. Mamma G and Fran's father had divorced, so she didn't want her daughter to struggle like she did.

Plus, Mamma G was a Christian and didn't believe in divorce. Fran didn't want to deal with her mother's judgment of her life decisions, so she kept the divorce a secret. After her marriage was legally dissolved, she would accept Mel's offer to move into his new townhome. It seemed like the best move for her and Calvin. She hoped to begin a beautiful chapter in her life in a new relationship with Mel.

Fran wasted no time. A month after her divorce was finalized, she and Calvin moved in with Mel. Her mom didn't approve of her shacking up and being in a relationship with an older man, but Fran had made up her mind. Every once in a while, Fran's intuition told her that Mamma G was right, but she was sure everything would be fine. He only wanted to take care of her and Calvin. Mel had proven that time after time by treating them like family for over a year.

Fran was ready to begin a new chapter in her life. On the weekends, they enjoyed eating dinner as a family, going to the park, and driving around downtown Lincoln on Sundays. Mel brought her flowers or a small gift on Fridays just because. He took her to a play and dinner for her birthday. Not a day went by without Mel letting Fran know that she was beautiful.

Fran and Calvin quickly settled into their new home with Mel. They had plenty of room to move around in the 3-bedroom multi-level townhome on the corner of Lexington Street. Calvin decorated his new room with his favorite cartoon characters. Mel made them feel at home.

The neighborhood where Mel lived was unique. On one side of the street, there were people wandering aimlessly looking for jobs or hanging out on the corners. On the other side, people were dressed in their professional attire headed to work. It was unusual to see such opposite representations of African American families living in the city, but it made Fran appreciate what she had.

Six months later, everything changed. Fran didn't understand it, but Mel started treating her differently. One night, she overheard a phone conversation between him and some guy named Poncho. When he got off the phone, he came into the bedroom. He seemed nervous and afraid. It was if someone had threatened his life.

Fran noticed Mel's behavior had changed. He looked as though he was paranoid about something. Over the next few days, he no longer showered her with hugs or kisses. He went days without talking to her or Calvin, and he spent several nights sleeping on the couch.

Unable to keep herself from ignoring Mel's behavior, Fran decided to speak to him about it. One morning, she walked downstairs to the living room and confronted him. She asked what was wrong and why he slept on the couch. With a troubled look on his face, Mel dismissed her and said he had to go to work.

It was a cold and dark winter day on January 14, 1965 when Mel left and never returned home. The last time Fran spoke to him was the morning she confronted him. She suspected his disappearance had a lot to do with the mysterious phone call she had overheard. Being 8 months pregnant, she couldn't believe she was in the same predicament again. She was left hurt and abandoned by a man.

Concerned something had happened to Mel, Fran called the car dealership to speak to his manager, Mr. Redford. She told Mr. Redford she was his fiancé and asked if he had arrived at work. Mr. Redford told her that he hadn't seen Mel in a few days and was wondering if he was okay. Fran's heart dropped. She became worried something tragic had happened to him.

Not knowing where it came from, the thought crossed Fran's mind that Mel could be living a double life. Reflecting on her life since she moved to Lincoln, she asked herself why she attracted men who abandoned her. Could abandonment be a repeated cycle or a generational curse? In that moment, Fran thought back to her mother's words about shacking up with a man. She didn't want to admit that her mother was right.

Fran didn't know what to do. Fears of being a single mom and providing for her children made her feel anxious all over again. How could she take care of two children with one income? Charles' child support payments were sporadic, and she didn't know if Mel would ever come back home. She knew she could always go to her mother's house, but that wasn't the best option. Instead, she contemplated moving into her own place.

Every day, it seemed like her life was falling apart. First, Mel abandoned her, then the utilities were turned off. Fran knocked on a neighbor's door to use their phone. She called the power company to determine how much was owed. The representative told her the power bill hadn't been paid in six months. Then, she called the telephone company to restore service. When she found out the outstanding balance, Fran was upset. She knew she couldn't pay both companies and the mortgage. Both companies had refused to restore services until the balances were paid in full.

Fran had assumed Mel was being responsible with the money she contributed towards the bills. Fortunately, like her mother, she had stashed cash from each paycheck under her mattress for a rainy day. Her mother always told her, "Don't let your left hand know what your right hand is doing." Fran interpreted it to mean to not let any man think she was totally financially dependent on him.

Mamma G taught Fran to always have an escape plan just in case things didn't work out. With the $200 cash she hid from Mel, Fran bought enough food to make it through the next few weeks. If she didn't hear from Mel, she would swallow her pride and ask to move back in with her mom. With another baby on the way, Fran would also benefit from the help her mother could provide.

One night, lying on the striped burgundy and black couch in the living room, Fran and Calvin bundled under a couple of blankets. The temperature dropped below 30 degrees. Calvin asked Fran where Mel was. It was hard for her to respond without getting emotional. She hoped he would walk through the door to restore their family at any minute. Since she didn't respond to Calvin, he asked her again when Mel would be home.

Cuddling closer to him, Fran told her son that Mel was out of town and would be home soon. Fran got up from the couch to light a small candle and placed it on the brown square coffee table. After Calvin fell asleep, Fran cried. Her fear of being a single parent again had become her reality. The baby was due in a few weeks, and thinking about all of her financial responsibilities kept her up all night.

The next day, she called her mother and asked if she could move back home. Fran knew she would have to listen to her mom's lecture about the consequences of shacking up with a man. Her mother loved to remind her that there was no point in buying the cow when the milk was free. Mamma G told Fran that she shouldn't keep giving her body to men without a commitment. She didn't want to listen to her mom when it came to making life decisions.

Two weeks went by and there had been no word from Mel. Fran asked her older brother, Van, if he could help her move back into Mamma G's house. Her brother lived in Brookville, New York. Van had moved with their father, William, when the family was separated. After he graduated from high school, he joined the Army. Fran didn't see Van much, but they kept in touch through letters and phone calls. Van looked out for all of his sisters.

The drive from Brookville to Lincoln was four hours. Van pulled up in his light blue Chevy pickup truck. Calvin was so happy to see him. "Uncle Van. Uncle Van!" Calvin exclaimed as he jumped into his uncle's arms. "Have you been a good boy?" Van asked him.

His friend, Victor, had tagged along to help when Van told him Fran was in trouble. She explained to her brother that Mel had left her and Calvin in his home and hadn't returned. She was expecting a baby in a few weeks, so she couldn't depend on him to take care of his responsibilities. Van said he didn't respect any man who walked out on a woman or his child. Van called Mel a bum.

MEET MY BROTHER, CALVIN

Calvin Eugene Davis was born in Lincoln City, Maryland on May 13, 1959 to Fran and Charles Davis. My mother told me that when he was in the 3rd grade, one of his classmates, Clinton Johnson, gave him the nickname "Shorty" because he was the shortest kid in Mrs. Olderman's class. The next summer, she said Calvin had a growth spurt and was taller than all of his classmates. Regardless, his peers kept calling him by his nickname.

When we were young, I remembered when Calvin played sports with his friends in front of the apartment building. He was a great athlete and was a center on the basketball team at Lincoln Middle School. At the end of his basketball season, he joined the recreation football league. That year, he led the Old Town Tigers football team to their first championship.

Growing up with Calvin, I had a lot of fond memories of him. He usually got on my nerves. At times, he tried to boss me around and tell me what to do. I was 7, and he was 13. Every day after school, he used to babysit me and took pleasure in torturing and forcing me to do his chores. If I refused, he wouldn't let me go outside.

Calvin used to call me a tattletale, but I didn't care. Every time he played hooky from school, didn't wash the dishes, or smoked cigarettes in the apartment, I told on him. When he tried to bribe me, I still told my mom everything he had done. As soon as my mom walked through the door I'd say, "Mom, Calvin had some girls over here when you told him he couldn't have company!"

Every time he got in trouble, I hid behind my door and laughed at him. My mom scolded him and punished him for a week. Walking past my room, he would give me a mean look while balling up his fist at me. I was scared he would beat me up. He promised that he would hit me and I believed him.

I remember the Sunday when it was my turn to set the table for dinner, Calvin groaned because he had to wash the dishes. Rolling his eyes at me, he got up from the table and lunged at me like he was going to punch me in the face. I jumped out of my seat afraid he would hit me. I screamed out and told my mom Calvin had threatened me. She came out of her room fussing and warned him to leave me alone. If he didn't, he would be in more trouble.

Even though he irked my nerves, I knew my brother loved me. He always teased me by calling me "Boney." I hated when he called me that. Every time he tormented me, I wanted to punch him. Once, he said I was ugly, so I hurled a shoe at him. He found a boot and threw it back at me. I ran towards him with both of my fists balled up tight to punch him in the face. I started swinging my arms like a pinwheel, closing my eyes until he pushed me flat on the floor. He won the fight. We both laughed.

My brother was smart, but he hung out with the wrong crowd. To him, his friends were his family, so he looked to them for guidance. Most of his friends lived in a single-parent home with their moms and no sign of a man around. From skipping school to smoking pot, my brother was always in trouble. The school called to complain that he missed several days of classes.

My mom couldn't find a role model or mentor for him. She reached out to several community organizations for young black males but didn't receive any help. Uncle Van, lived four hours away in New York. He was the only male figure in Calvin's life. He called Calvin once a month to give him a lecture and encouraged him to stay out of trouble. Every once in a while, his father Charles, made a cameo appearance.

For his 15th birthday, Calvin asked my mom if he could have a telephone in his room. She gave in because he had stretched out the white spiral phone cord in the kitchen. Every night, Calvin talked on the phone to his classmates from school. Rapping and mouthing a bunch of fibs to the girls was what he did best. I heard him through the bedroom walls saying all sorts of untruths.

Our bedrooms were right next to each other, so I would often put a clear drinking glass up against the wall to catch every word he said. If

Calvin's voice sounded muffled, I sat outside of his door to eavesdrop on his conversations. I heard him talking to his girlfriends, adding bass to his voice. "What's up, slim? Girl, you know I like you. I can't stop thinking about you." Ten minutes later, he'd hang up and dial his next victim. He told her the same lines he told the other girl. They all fell for his lies and believed him.

MEET EBONI

I will never forget the day when I was 12 years old and my mom recounted everything about what happened the day I was born. Every aspect of the day was special and worth retelling from the time she went into labor until I was handed to her.

She described the morning when her water broke. She screamed out to my grandmother, Mamma G, that she was in labor. Mamma G didn't drive, so she called her friend, Ms. Ruth, to take her to Lincoln City Regional Community Hospital. Calvin was excited about being a big brother. Ms. Ruth pulled up in her red 1963 Chevy. Ms. Ruth blew her horn to let them know she was outside. She said she kissed Calvin goodbye and told him she would be home with me, his baby sister, in a couple of days.

Moving as fast as she could, my mom said she wobbled down the steps holding her stomach. She got in the car and held on for dear life, praying she would make it to the hospital in time. The contractions were 10 minutes apart. She told me she was in a lot of pain.

Ruth dropped her off in front of the emergency room doors. Holding onto her stomach, she got out of the car. My father, Mel, was nowhere to be found. She said she hadn't seen or heard from him since the day he left in January.

I was born on March 10, 1965 at 6:26 PM. I was 21 inches long and weighed 6 pounds and 3 ounces. My mom said she hadn't decided on my name yet, but she was so happy I was a girl. After the nurses cleaned me up and put me in the baby bassinet, she asked if she could hold me.

Before handing me to her, the nurse and doctor hesitated. My mom said they looked concerned. She saw them huddled around me whispering. When she asked them if something was wrong, the orthopedic specialist explained to her that my right foot was deformed. Unsure of what he was saying, she asked the doctor to clarify.

The physician recommended they perform surgery and put a cast on my right foot. My mom said she started crying because she was worried, I was in pain. She thought my foot was permanently fixed in a curved position, which made her upset. After explaining everything to my mom, the nurses finally handed me to her.

Opening the baby blanket, she was in shock. Dr. Brin, the orthopedic surgeon, assured her that I would be fine and walking normal before I turned 3 years old. He told her that they would put a corrective brace on my foot after the cast was removed. Mom kissed me on my cheek, then wrapped me up before she gave me to the surgeon.

After my surgery, my mom said the doctor discharged her. With a cast on my right foot all the way up to my knee, she dressed me in a cute pink and white dress. Ms. Ruth was en route to pick us up. Waiting inside by the hospital door, my mom couldn't wait to go home. When Ms. Ruth pulled up, she had a big smile on her face. She removed the blanket and took a good look at me. Then, she congratulated my mom on giving birth to a precious little baby girl.

Calvin stood waiting at the front door excited to see me when Ms. Ruth pulled up to Mamma G's building. "I want to name her Eboni," my brother said. When my mom walked through the door, she acknowledged Calvin's request. "Are you naming her after your little girlfriend, Ebony?" He blushed and said, "Yes."

Torn between embracing me or his new litter of brown puppies, my mom asked Calvin if he could hold me while she fixed my bottle. After holding me in his arms and rocking me to sleep, she relieved my brother of his babysitting duties. Then, he rushed to the porch to tend to his dog, Duchess and her puppies.

It was a celebration the day my mom brought me home from the hospital. Mamma G set the table for dinner. Calvin reminded my mom that he wanted to name me after Ebony, a little girl who lived on the second floor. My mom described her as a cute brown skin little girl with dimples and thick long hair.

Mamma G said I was so spoiled because I was the only baby in the house. Whenever I cried, someone was always there to pick me up and console me. When no one was watching, I crawled around the apartment at record speeds. Calvin couldn't keep up with me. At 10 months, I took my first step with the white cast on my foot. Everyone was excited I could walk.

My mother told me my corrective brace was removed when I was 2 years old. At a follow up consultation with Dr. Brin, he said my foot seemed to be back in its natural position, so he removed the metal brace. Mamma G said I paraded around the apartment when I got home from the doctor's office. I walked from room to room. Everyone watched and cheered me on as I discovered my newfound freedom, no longer having to wear the brace.

2
IN THE MIDDLE

RELIGION

Mamma G was the apple of my eye. She was a dedicated, tithing, and faithful member of Mt. Lebanon Baptist Church. The church was located on Linden Place in Lincoln City, MD. Mt. Lebanon Baptist was a popular place of worship for African American families in the Lincoln community.

Calvin and I attended church with Mamma G every Sunday. When we spent the night on Saturday nights at Mamma G's, we had to go to church with her on Sunday mornings. Mamma G practically stayed in church because she belonged to several ministries. On Mondays, she went to prayer meetings, on Wednesdays she attended nurse's ministry meetings, and on Fridays she met with the usher board.

I loved spending time with Mamma G on Sunday mornings because she fixed the best Sunday morning breakfast. It was one of the reasons why I liked to stay over on Saturday nights. Every Sunday, she cooked a delicious breakfast with pancakes, scrapple, biscuits, bacon, scrapple and eggs. I watched her cook in the kitchen, whipping up pancakes from scratch. Flour, baking soda, milk, and eggs were the ingredients of her famous pancakes.

She'd pull out a yellow bowl and mix the ingredients. She sifted the flour in a silver-like container with a net, squeezing the handle as the flour went into the bowl. The bacon and scrapple were fried in her black cast iron skillet on the gas stove. Mmmmmmm. The aroma of the bacon made my stomach growl. Meanwhile, the egg yolks were in another glass bowl sitting on the counter.

When Mamma G cooked, she sang along to the spirituals that played on the gospel AM radio station. Tuned to her favorite gospel station on WBL AM, she sang the words to "Soon and Very Soon." She'd sing, swaying from side to side to the music. Then, she got "happy" pulling out her pink handkerchief to wipe the tears from her eyes. Mamma G was moved by the lyrics of the spirituals and shouted, "Thank you, Jesus," when the song was over.

When I was a little girl, my mom bought me the cutest Sunday dresses that were frilly, colorful, and had lots of bows. She made me wear black patent leather shoes with white frilly socks, and she fixed my hair into a ponytail adorned with bows that matched my dress. Calvin wore a dark blue suit, white dress shirt, and tie.

When we walked in the church, the aroma of fried chicken filled up every room. Every Sunday, the usher board ministry held a fundraiser in the fellowship hall, located in the basement of the church. They sold fried chicken dinners with macaroni and cheese, green beans, and sweet potato pie or pound cake for dessert. The dinners were $5. All of the proceeds from the sales, provided scholarships for the youth, and funded other church events.

Service started promptly at 11:00 am, and it was supposed to end at 1:00 pm. Sometimes, service didn't end until 2:00 pm. It was painful sitting for hours on those long brown benches in the pews. Church service seemed like it would never end. Mamma G was never phased by the number of hours we stayed in church.

Church usually began with an opening hymn, a solo from one of the choir members, three songs from the sanctuary choir, the morning announcements, visitor acknowledgments, and a scripture reading. Sometimes, I got up to stretch my legs, telling Mamma G I had to go to the bathroom or that something was in my eye. There were times when I fell asleep before the pastor started preaching and woke up during the altar call.

At 8 years old, I joined the youth usher board ministry. I wanted to be an usher just like Mamma G. Deacon Brown was in charge. He taught us how to usher the members in and out of the sanctuary during service. It wasn't until I became an usher that I realized there was a unique system of communicating. Deacon Brown gave me a book with all the codes, gestures and rules. Rule number one was that ushers were supposed to stand in their positions for at least 15 minutes. To me, that was a long time to stand, but I wanted to make Mamma G proud.

My best friend, Tish, was on the usher board. She was a little taller than me, with a light brown complexion and short hair. We met in Sister Johnson's Sunday School class and were the same age. She went to church with her grandmother every Sunday like I did.

Deacon Brown said Tish and I could take a 15-minute break. We couldn't wait to go downstairs and act like the sanctified ladies of the church. Standing in front of the bathroom mirror, we took turns pretending to fall out like the ladies in church. "Thank ya, Lord! Thank ya, Jesus! " Tish would say before she imitated one of the church ladies passing out.

Then, Tish would fall back into my arms as I fanned her. "Sister Tish! Are you okay?" I'd ask her. Then, she'd jump up and start running around the bathroom like she was getting "happy." Getting "happy" in the black church is when you felt the spirit of the Holy Ghost. It made you want to dance. We both started laughing. Suddenly, someone would knock on the bathroom door. It was usually Sister Mitchell.

"What y'all doing in there?" She'd say.

"Nothing, Sister Mitchell," we'd respond in unison.

Quickly, we ran back upstairs to the sanctuary because our break was over.

One Sunday morning, the youth ushers lined up on each side of the pews in the church. Deacon Brown taught us how to direct people to their seats using hand signals and gestures. If a member wanted to leave the sanctuary, the usher put the index and middle finger together directing the member to exit the church.

By the 4th Sunday, I knew all the secret codes and hand signals. I was surprised I remembered them all. Deacon Brown showed me how to point my right index finger to show one seat was available in the last pew. Both pointed index fingers meant two seats were available in the last row of the pew. If I placed my fist over my heart, it meant I was supposed to stand in position for 15 more minutes.

Placing my right hand on my shoulder meant it was time to be relieved from my position. If an usher was standing in position at the pew, holding their hands behind their back, it meant to wait until Deacon Brown directed you to move. Being an usher was hard work, especially memorizing all of the codes and hand signals.

The sanctified ladies at Mt. Lebanon made me laugh. They were funny and very entertaining to watch. They dressed in their Sunday best every week. Wearing big hats, bright colored dresses, and lots of perfume, they pranced into the sanctuary as if there was a celebration. Before the sermon was over, the ladies always got "happy" and danced around the church.

Church service became even more interesting once I began paying attention. I never noticed members running around the sanctuary, dancing, or shouting during the pastor's sermons. It was probably because I was asleep. When Mamma G got "happy," but she didn't dance around the church. She just cried and fanned herself.

When the sanctified ladies got the Holy Ghost, they danced around at their seats. Since Mamma G was also a member of the nurse's ministry. The nurses waited in the back; ready to assist and guard the sanctified ladies. They stood ready to assist members who got "happy" or filled with the Holy Ghost. Mamma G and the nurses were ready for anything that happened.

One Sunday, Mamma Sheila got happy. During the sermon, Mamma Sheila jumped around at her seat. Mamma G and the other nurses formed a circle around her. Tish and I didn't understand her gibberish or what she was saying. They said she was "speaking in tongues." It sounded like a foreign language to me.

Mamma Sheila was an older lady in the church, around 70 years old. A tall, pretty lady who smelled like roses, she'd always strut her stuff and look around to see if anyone was watching her. Mamma Sheila had no problem showing off her brand-new blue hat, bright blue dress, blue shoes, and fancy blue gloves. Before she sat in her seat, she'd walk around the sanctuary waiting for people to give her compliments.

Tish and I called her "the blue lady" because she wore a different shade of blue every Sunday. Right before the sermon, like clockwork, Mamma Sheila would stand up and shout and speak in tongues. The nurse's ministry stood by to make sure she didn't fall out on the floor. They fanned and comforted her. Eventually, she sat back down in her seat.

Before the anniversary service began, Pastor Lewis asked the congregation to stand as the ushers prepared to march down the middle aisle of the sanctuary. It was Mt. Lebanon's Usher Board 9th anniversary. Dressed in her usher uniform, Mamma G smiled as she marched in sync with the usher board members to my favorite song, "I'm Goin' Up" by Walter Hawks.

Clapping and singing down the aisle, they were dressed in their all-white dresses, hats, stockings, and shoes. The church members stood waiting in the pews as the ushers marched in a two-step cadence down the aisle of the sanctuary, swaying from left to right. Marching to the reserved section up front, the ushers sat in the first three rows because it was their special day.

Once service was over, Tish and I were off from usher duty. We hugged each other and said our goodbyes. Mamma G, my mom, and my brother picked up our dinners from the fellowship hall. As we were leaving, we heard a lady yelling in the front of the church. It was Mamma Sheila.

She was upset and cursing at Deacon Larry. Being nosy, I walked closer to Mamma Sheila so that I could hear. Why was Mamma Sheila fussing with Deacon Larry? Deacon Larry walked fast, practically running to get to his car and away from her. Mamma Sheila yelled, "You no good, son of a gun, dog!" Deacon Larry, looked down in shame and didn't say a word. He kept walking toward his car. I asked Mamma G, "Why is Mamma Sheila fussing at Deacon Larry?"

"Stay out of grown folks' business," she said. I left it alone.

After service, we walked back to Mamma G's apartment and ate our dinners. My grandmother said I could spend the night because I didn't have school on Monday. She told me to ask for my mom's permission to stay over. My mom said that I could.

Mamma G decorated her entire apartment in pink, her favorite color. The walls were painted in a pastel pink and her queen-sized bed was decorated with round pink pillows. She had pink square pillows on the pink chairs in her bedroom. Taking it a step further, Mamma G had a pink lamp on her night stand. Her room was a beautiful pink palace that smelled like a pink petunia flower.

My mom and Calvin went home before dark. Even though Mamma G said I could stay, I had to go to bed at 8:00 pm. When it was almost bedtime, I took my bath, put on my pajamas and robe, and combed my hair. Afraid of the dark, I didn't couldn't fall asleep. Calvin always told me the Boogeyman was going to get me.

I laid in the bed with the lights on until my grandmother came in the room. It was 8:00 pm, so Mamma G told me to turn off the lights. Then, she kissed me on my forehead. I tossed and turned; I couldn't fall asleep. Finally, I pulled her beautiful pink blanket over my head.

Lying in the bed and being afraid of the dark made me think about Mamma G's sister, Eva, who had died a few weeks earlier. It was my first time going to a funeral and seeing a family member in a casket. My grandmother cried, and that made me sad knowing that one day she too would die. The day of her sister's funeral, Mamma G cried all day long. I couldn't help myself.

I just blurted out how I was feeling. "Mamma G, I'm afraid of dying. I don't want to die Mamma G!"

Sitting on the edge of the bed, she hugged me.

Holding me in her arms, she said, "Eboni, God is with you, and he will never leave you." She continued, "Eboni do you know the Lord's Prayer?"

Sitting on the edge of the bed, she asked me to repeat after her. "Our Father who art in heaven, hallowed be thy name." "Our Father, who art in heaven, hallowed be thy name." I repeated every line of the prayer with Mamma G.

I felt better, but I asked Mamma G if I could keep the light on. She said that I could keep it on for a little while. Her phone rang, so she got up to answer it. I could see her on the phone in the living room. Mamma G chuckled with one of her girlfriends. I listened to her conversation until I fell asleep.

The following Sunday, on September 13, 1975, after Sunday school service, I was baptized in the basement of Mt. Lebanon Baptist Church. Tish, Isaiah, and Linda from Sunday School were also being baptized that day. For my baptism, I wore a white dress, black patent shoes, and frilly socks my mother bought me.

Baptisms were held on the 1st Sunday of the month, Before the ceremony, everyone who was being baptized lined up next to the baptismal font, a big, wide metal bowl of water. Our Sunday School teacher, Sister Johnson, gave us white sheets with sleeves as; our baptismal outfits. Before the baptism ceremony, the deacons, teachers, and members sang hymns. Pastor Lewis asked everyone to remain seated in their chairs when the ceremony began. I didn't want to get my hair wet because my mom had washed and pressed it the night before.

Pastor Lewis walked up the metal steps and stepped into the pool of water wearing his black robe. Then, he called my name. I walked up the metal steps, holding on to the metal railing with my right hand. My left hand held my gown to keep my underwear from showing.

Sister Johnson told me I would become a new creature in Christ when I got baptized. Pastor reached for my hand as I stepped into the cold baptismal pool of water. With his left hand behind my back and the other hand holding my arm, Pastor Lewis said, "Eboni Antoinette, I am baptizing you in the name of Jesus Christ."

I pinched my nose with my right hand before he dunked me in the water. Pastor Lewis dunking me underwater symbolized me being washed clean of my sins. He lifted me back up to stand as I wiped the cold water from my eyes. One of the deacons reached for my hand to help me step out of the pool. Sister Johnson was waiting to help me walk down the steps.

The rest of my friends lined up ready to be baptized. I didn't feel any different afterwards. I felt the same, even though Sister Johnson said I would be brand new. I put my church clothes back on in the bathroom. Sister Johnson handed me a bag that had a big white book wrapped with a bow. The title of the book was "Living the Ten Commandments." Sister Johnson signed the inside cover of my book. She congratulated me on getting baptized.

After my baptism, Mamma G made sure I went to church with her every Sunday. Sometimes, my mom worked at her part-time job on Sundays, so we didn't make it to church. Calvin never liked going to church. If we didn't go to church with Mamma G, Calvin and I went to Mt. Zion Baptist. The young adults of Mt. Zion's ministry picked up kids from our apartment complex every Sunday in a white school bus.

One of the youth leaders drove the bus, and they picked up about 20 kids from my neighborhood. The youth leaders were white, but they seemed to like black kids. The young men and women looked like they were in their late teens or early twenties. On our way to church, we sang songs. I loved to sing. One of my favorites was the Bible song. I'll never forget the words: "The B-I-B-L-E, yes that's the book for me. I stand alone on the Word of God, the B-I-B-L-E."

The youth leaders shared their testimonies and taught us lessons about Jesus Christ. On the way home, we earned a prize if we followed the bus rules. The youth leaders also gave a prize to the person who could quote the scripture verse of the day. I sat quietly reading the church pamphlets they gave me. I wanted to win the prize badly. For some reason, they never picked me when I raised my hand to recite the verse. Even though the prize was a pencil or a piece of candy, I still wanted to win.

THE COLOR OF MY SKIN

After being baptized and becoming a new creature in Christ, I thought life was supposed to be easier. Every day was a good day. I didn't feel like a new creature; I felt the opposite. I hated my life and the color of my skin. I felt ugly. And I didn't know why I was so ugly. I asked my mom why Calvin's complexion was lighter than mine. She didn't respond.

My mother and brother were both a lighter complexion than me. Mamma G could almost pass for being white. There were many shades of black in my family, which confused me. What happened to me? Was I adopted? When I looked in the mirror, I hated my little pug nose, small lips, and beady eyes.

Most of my friends were a few shades lighter than me. They often reminded me all the time that I was the darker one in the group. During the summer, family members told me to stay out of the sun. They'd ask me why I was so black. I didn't know why I was so dark. Being a darker-skinned black girl felt like a curse.

Sometimes, my friends, teachers, and even family members ignored me because I was too dark for their liking. Feeling small and irrelevant, I didn't think I mattered. On most days, I felt unworthy and like I was not enough. It hurt to be teased by my family and peers. I especially didn't like when they called me "blackie" or "darkie," as if black was a bad color.

I remembered the day at recess being black got me in trouble. My first and last fist fight was on October 4, 1974. We were on the playground lined up to play kickball. Kim, Sharon, and I were waiting for our turn to kick the ball. Already on first, second, and third base, Keith, and Jay were ready to run to home base. It was my turn to kick the ball.

Deborah came over out of nowhere, got in front of me, and pushed me on the ground. She wanted to get in front of me in line. My friend,

Sharon, helped me up and asked if I was ok. Deborah and I were in the same grade, but she was white. I knew she didn't like me. I heard she didn't like black people.

Because Deborah was taller than me, she thought she could beat me up. I had to confront her for pushing me on the ground. There was dirt on my new red striped jumpsuit my mother bought me from Montgomery Place. Deborah stood in the kickball line laughing with one of her friends.

I got up enough courage to confront her. "Deborah, why did you push me and butt in line?"

"You need to go to the back of the line, nigger!" Deborah said. "You belong in the back of the line."

My heart was beating fast. With my eyes closed, tears rolling down my face, and my fist balled up tight, I punched Deborah in the face. I opened my eyes after I punched her. With blood running down her face, Deborah held her nose. She started crying and ran toward Ms. Green, one of the teachers in charge during recess.

Looking back and pointing at me, she told the teacher I punched her in the nose. She and Ms. Green started walking toward me. Deborah was holding her nose with a tissue to wipe the blood dripping from her nose. I panicked. Ms. Green didn't ask any questions. She assumed I was guilty of punching Deborah in the nose. I started to explain what happened.

Ms. Green didn't want to hear what I had to say. She told me I had to go to the principal's office. She grabbed my arm as if I was a criminal. Ms. Green was mad. If she had allowed me to tell her Deborah called me a nigger, she would have understood why I punched her. Being escorted to the principal's office, everyone stared at me in trouble.

I didn't know if I was going to be suspended or kicked out of school. No one would believe that it wasn't my fault and that Deborah called me a nigger. Sitting in the principal's office, I saw Deborah being escorted to the nurse's office. The teachers and staff treated her like she was the victim.

With tears falling as I sat waiting for Principal Davis to return to his office, I hoped he wouldn't hold this incident against me. I was a straight-A student, served on safety patrol, and was liked by my teachers. No one wanted to hear my side of the story.

Principal Davis was tall and intimidating. He walked around the hallways with a mean look on his face. Most of the students were afraid of him. They called him "Lurch" because he was at least seven feet tall. He didn't tolerate bad behavior, especially fighting. When he walked the hallways, students displayed their best behavior. Scared out of my mind and afraid my mother would kill me; I knew I would be grounded for at least a year.

I had been waiting for at least 20 minutes, but Principal Davis was still in a meeting. The anticipation was killing me. I should have told Ms. Green that Deborah called me the n-word. Ms. Green is African American, she would have understood why I punched her.

As far as I was concerned, Deborah calling me the n-word confirmed she didn't like black people. I didn't mean to make her nose bleed. Deborah should know better than to call a black person a nigger. I hoped Principal Davis would give me a light sentence after I told him what happened.

When Principal Davis walked in his office, he said, "Eboni, what's going on?" I stuttered, "Principal Davis, Deborah pushed me on the ground and called me a nigger. She told me to go to the back of the line." I asked him, "It's not right when white people call black people the n-word, right?"

His countenance changed. He paused and pulled out a piece of pink paper from his desk. Was he going to suspend me? I started crying. He handed me a piece of tissue to wipe my eyes. I could tell he felt sorry for me after I explained what happened on the playground.

After I wiped my eyes, he explained that he understood why I punched Deborah. Then, he advised me against fighting. "Eboni, I don't approve of you punching Deborah, but I understand how it made you feel. I've been called a nigger before. Don't resort to violence when someone calls you out of your name." He continued, "The next time anyone calls you out of your name, make sure you let your teacher know. We will deal with them."

I promised Principal Davis that I would tell a teacher the next time someone called me the n-word. "Eboni, I know you are a good student. You can go back to class. Wipe the tears from your eyes," he said. While handing me a pink piece of paper with his signature on it, Principal Davis smiled and told me to have a good day.

My day was already better. I walked into my class. My friends were proud of me for standing up to Deborah. Kim asked if I had gotten suspended, and I told her I hadn't. I made up my mind that I wouldn't tell my mom what happened in school, unless she brought it up.

In July of 1975, my mom said that I could attend a Christian camp, Teen Jump, in Stinton, Pennsylvania. The youth camp was sponsored by Mt. Zion Baptist Church. This was the same church that picked up kids in my apartment complex every Sunday. Every summer, Mt. Zion sponsored over 30 kids to attend a youth camp.

The week-long camp was more like a spiritual retreat for youth ages 10 to 18. Excited to go to camp, I packed my bags a week early. I enjoyed going to the church, so I knew camp would be a lot of fun. The same white young adults who picked me up for church drove the white school bus to Teen Jump.

There were 20 kids piled on the bus headed to camp. We left the church at 8:00 am, and we arrived at Teen Jump by 11:00 am. Getting off the bus, I saw at least 100 kids arriving at the same time. Kids were running around the beautiful campsite when they got off the school bus.

The landscape of the campsite was beautiful. It looked like something in a magazine. The manicured lawns and flowers enhanced the landscape of the site. Two-level brown log cabins spread across the campsite. At the top of the hill was a small church. There was an Olympic-size swimming pool on the side of a red brick building.

The counselors gave us our cabin numbers before we got off the bus. They instructed us to take our belongings to the cabin. I made a new friend on the bus, Robin. We ended up being assigned to the same cabin. We were the same age. Robin lived in Averton, Virginia. Her dad was a pastor of a church in Lincoln City.

We took our things to the cabin, then the counselors gave us free time to swim at the pool. Robin put on her bathing suit in five minutes flat. I asked her to wait for me. Looking through my luggage, I had to find my bathing suit and swimming cap. I didn't want to mess up my hair. My mom would be mad if my hair got wet because I had a perm.

Walking over to the pool, we met some girls our age. We all walked to the pool together. As soon as we entered the gate, we threw our towels on the long chairs and jumped in. My swimming cap came off, but I didn't care because I wanted to swim and have fun with my new friends. Deciding to just enjoy myself, I threw my swimming cap on the chair.

My new friends and I played around in the pool for an hour until lunchtime. After lunch, we walked over to the administration building. Our counselor told us we could do arts and crafts at 3:00 pm. The counselors taught us how to paint beautiful designs on rocks. Robin and I finished painting our rocks and went back to our cabin to get dressed for dinner.

Around 5:30 pm, the counselors told everyone to form a circle for our devotional in the main building of the campsite. The theme of the camp was "We are the Light." The teen counselors started the devotional time with praise and worship songs. We sang one of my favorite songs, "Kumbaya My Lord."

Then, the counselors helped us memorize a scripture Matthew 5:14-16: "Ye are the light of the world. A city that is set on a hill cannot be hid. Neither do men light a candle and put it under a bushel, but on a candlestick; and it giveth light unto all that are in the house. Let your light so shine before men, that they may see your good deeds and glorify your Father in heaven" (KJV).

On the first night of our devotional service, I felt different. It was a feeling I couldn't describe. I felt a sense of peace. The youth leaders shared their testimonies and talked about how having a relationship with Christ had impacted their lives. Their testimonies and the songs we sang made me want to know Jesus more than I ever had before.

The youth stood up one by one to share their thoughts about Jesus Christ. I was touched by their testimonies, but I was too shy to stand up. Robin wasn't shy. She shared her testimony about prayer. Her mother had been diagnosed with cancer, and the doctor told her that she only had six months to live.

Robin said she prayed with her mom every day that God would heal her. She started crying. I gave her a piece of tissue to wipe her eyes. Her biological father had died when she was three years old. When Robin sat down, I gave her a hug. Everyone in the circle started crying. We all comforted and hugged one another.

After the devotional, we walked outside to roast marshmallows over the campfire. We sang more praise and worship songs until it got dark, around 9:00 pm. Our counselor, Ms. Lisa had us all gather together to walk back to our cabin. It was dark outside, so we used our flashlights to find our way back.

In the middle of the night, I started having chills. One minute I was hot, and the next I was cold. It felt like I was coming down with the flu. I kept covering and uncovering myself with my sleeping bag. I told Ms. Lisa that I didn't feel well. She got up from her bed and felt my head to see if I had a fever. I had a temperature of 101 degrees.

She gave me medicine from her first aid kit. I felt a little better, but I had a fever again the next morning. I had to stay in bed until the following morning. While the other girls in the cabin went to breakfast, I was stuck in bed with flu-like symptoms.

Ms. Lisa stayed in the cabin with me. At 10:30 am, she helped me climb out of bed and escorted me to the nurse's office. The nurse took my temperature; it read higher than 101 degrees on the thermometer. She gave me more medicine, then told me to lie down in her office for a few hours.

As I was preparing to doze off, I heard the nurse talking to my mom, letting her know I was sick with the flu. She assured her she would continue to give me medicine and monitor my progress. I missed out on the fun the girls were having at camp. Robin stopped by to see me in the nurse's office after breakfast. Ms. Lisa also came by to check on me.

By dinner, I felt well enough to eat and go to devotional. By Thursday afternoon, I felt much better. I went to the pool and participated in all the camp activities. My favorite part of camp was arts and crafts. Robin made me a cute purple gimp necklace. She helped me tie it around my neck.

On the last night of camp, at devotional, Ms. Lisa my counselor shared her testimony. She was 21 years old. Ms. Lisa said she once hated God. When her little brother died in his sleep, he was 6 years old. She blamed God for his death.

When her brother died, she didn't understand why he died so young. After years of mourning his death and talking with her pastor, she realized that God had a plan for everyone. The room got quiet; you could barely hear a pin drop. One by one, we got up and gave Ms. Lisa a hug, even the other counselors. After hearing her testimony, I couldn't wait to get home and hug my family.

After the devotional time ended, everyone walked to the campfire and roasted marshmallows. Afterwards, we headed back to our cabins to pack our bags. We would be going home in the morning. I felt better and wanted to go home. I missed my mom, Mamma G, and Calvin.

Since it was our last night of camp, the other girls in the cabin and I played games with our flashlights. We flashed each other in the eyes and made funny animal figures with our fingers on the cabin walls. We giggled, laughed, and had fun while Ms. Lisa went to the camp leaders' meeting. We had a blast while she was gone.

An hour later, we heard Ms. Lisa walking toward our cabin. Before she opened the cabin door, we turned off our flashlights and pretended like we were asleep. Robin started snoring. Ms. Lisa wasn't fooled. She told us she knew we weren't asleep because she saw our flashlights had been on a few seconds before entering the cabin. We all laughed because we were busted.

Teen Jump camp was over. On the last day, Friday morning, we piled on the white school bus to head back home. I made a lot of friends at camp. Robin and I sat next to each other on the bus again. We sang songs we had learned and made up a few songs along the way.

Over and over again, we sang the Bingo song. We'd say, "B-I-N-G-O, B-I-N-G-O, and Bingo was his nam-o." Then, we sang the Bible song. We'd sing, "The B-I-B-L-E, that's the book for me." Next, was "This Little Light of Mine." We'd say, "I'm going to let it shine." We sang nonstop for two hours.

When the bus pulled into the parking lot, I saw my mom waiting for me. I gathered my sleeping bag and tote, then hugged Robin goodbye. As soon as I got off the bus, I ran to my mom. I was so happy to see her. She gave me a hug and asked if I had a good time. I told her that I had. I'm so glad I went to Teen Jump. I felt at peace and grew closer to Jesus Christ.

BEING FATHERLESS

I wore my favorite outfit to the end of the school year awards program at Old Town Elementary School. I wore a pink and white pleated striped skirt, a pink short- sleeve top with ruffles, and my jelly bean shoes because I wanted to look extra cute receiving my award. Most of my classmates had both of their parents at the award ceremony. The parents and students sat in the cafeteria waiting for the award ceremony to begin.

Watching my classmates walk into the cafeteria with their mothers and fathers made me jealous. I was jealous because they had both of their parents to celebrate their accomplishments. Their fathers walked in smiling and proud. Their fathers embraced them before they walked up to the podium to receive their awards. I didn't like not having a father. I never thought about asking my mother about his whereabouts.

My mom was proud of me. I had received several awards. I was safety patrol officer of the year, student of the year, and had received nothing less than "very good" on my report card. Most of the black kids' mothers and grandmothers attended the ceremony; their fathers weren't in the home. I guess what really mattered was that my family was there to support me.

Where was my father? The day of the ceremony I felt a void like never before. I missed something I never had. I had so many questions that no one would answer. Why wasn't my father in my life? I wanted to ask my mom during the ceremony, but I was afraid it would make her upset.

My mom was both father and mother. I know she did all that she could for me and Calvin. I wondered if my dad would have been proud if he knew about the awards I'd received at school. It would have been nice for him to be there to tell me that he was proud of me.

When I got home, I went to my bedroom. Looking in the mirror, I questioned why I looked the way I did. Who did I look like? Why didn't

I look like my mother, brother, or grandmother? Was my dark skin the reason my father ran away? Was I too ugly or too dark?

Why would a man bring a child into the world and leave? Every child, especially a daughter, needs the love of a father. I wasn't sure how to ask my mom about my father, but I wanted to know. What was his name? I was clueless.

The next day at recess, I asked my friends Kim, Jackie, Monique, and Sharon if they knew their dads. Kim and Jackie said they did. Sharon said she had never met her dad. Monique said her parents were divorced, so she didn't see her dad that often.

I asked Monique what she meant. She said it was what happened when parents decided to break up because they didn't like each other anymore. I wanted to ask her why she didn't see her dad. If her parents were divorced, had he broken up with her, too?

I just hoped that one day my dad would want to be a part of my life. If and when he came back, he'd come to me with his arms open wide and embrace me with his love. Then, he would apologize for not being there, promising he would never leave me again. I couldn't wait to meet him one day.

THE GAMES WE PLAYED

My mom, Calvin, and I lived at Everton Square Apartments. The apartment complex was filled with twenty 3-story brown buildings that stretched across two blocks down Everton Avenue. Everton Square is where many African American families in the city lived. There were only a handful of families from other cultures like Indian, Spanish, and European, that also lived there.

There was never a dull moment at Everton Square. Some of the neighborhood kids could stay outside after the street lights came on, but I couldn't. When I got home from school and finished my homework, I hung out with my friends. Both the boys and girls played jacks, marbles, hide-and-seek, kickball, hopscotch, Double Dutch, tennis, and Red Light/ Green Light. Calvin was always watching television or talking on the phone.

If I got on Calvin's nerves, he'd make me stay in the house until my mom got home from work. I'd tell him, "I've finished my homework, Calvin." He never checked it, anyway. I'd put on my "play clothes and shoes." Play clothes and shoes were what my mom told me to wear outside.

Every morning, she'd remind me to take off my school clothes and shoes before going outside so that I didn't mess them up. If she caught me outside in my school clothes or shoes, I would be punished for days. She only bought clothes and shoes at the beginning of the school year.

I yelled out to let Calvin know I was going outside and told him I would be right out front. I ran down the steps, opened the glass door, and jumped off the front steps to go meet my friends. By 4:00 pm, my friends were already outside waiting for me by the steps.

I met Sharon, Lema, Monique, and Lexi the first day we moved into our apartment. Monique, Lexi, and Sharon were brown just like me. Lema was Indian. We were all in the same grade at Old Town Elementary.

Walking to the playground, I asked Sharon, "Are you "grittin' on me?"

She laughed. "Eboni, are you grittin' on me?"

"Grittin on" someone was looking them up and down, scrutinizing what they looked like or what they had on.

"You wanna fight? I said.

Sharon responded, "Yes!"

We pretended to fight each other for a couple of minutes, tapping each other lightly with balled fists. Laughing at each other we would yell out "Sike!"

My friends and I all wanted to be cheerleaders one day. Lining up beside each other, we started our own cheer. Monique was the captain because she complained I wasn't loud enough. I could do a cartwheel and a walk-over, but she couldn't. The cheers were a series of beats we made with our feet.

Everyone knew the "Titty Bump" cheer. We never knew why it was called "Titty Bump." It went: "Titty bump, my name is Eboni, they call me Boney. Don't mess with me. Titty bump, titty bump." The four of us stomped our feet in sync to start the cheers, then I ended the cheer with a couple of cartwheels and a split.

The boys started walking toward us mimicking our cheers and beats. We knew they would come as soon as we started cheering. They mocked and imitated us, acting like girls by "joanin" on our beats. "Joanin" is when someone insults or makes fun of another. We quickly got used to it. Clapping their hands and stomping their feet, they tried to say our "Titty Bump" cheer. We laughed at them.

Jason was the only white boy in my building, and he had to get permission to hang out with the black boys from the complex. He liked hanging out with us and he thought he was so cool. The boys would sometimes allow him to play basketball with them at the court. Jason's family didn't approve of him hanging out with black kids.

We finished cheering and laughing with the boys. Then, we played hide-and-seek. Everyone placed their right foot together to form a circle. Nate led the eenie, meeni, miny, mo to determine who was "it." Nate's finger landed on Jason's foot, so he was "it." The boys had to find the girls first.

Hide-and-seek always turned into hide-and-go-get-it, which is when the boy caught the girl and kissed her. I only played hide-and-seek with the boys. I didn't want to be kissed. They didn't want to kiss me, anyway. They said I wasn't cute enough.

Sharon, the cutest girl in our bunch, had long hair, dimples, and a shapely body for an 11-year-old. The boys said she had a big butt. Some of the parents who lived in our building said Sharon was "fast," which meant she was mature and advanced for her age. They predicted she would be pregnant before she finished high school.

Jason and the boys leaned against the apartment building with their eyes closed, counting backwards from 10. Once they reached the number one, they said, "Ready or not, here we come." The boys wanted to kiss Sharon, so they looked for her first. I hid in the most obvious place, behind the bush in front of the building. They ran right past me.

Sharon always hid somewhere behind the building in her favorite hiding place. Jason couldn't find Monique, Lexi, or Lema, so he tagged me. He knew better than to try to kiss me. Eventually, the other boys came back, except Nate. One of the boys found Lexi behind a car, and Monique had been hiding behind a tall bush on the side of the building.

Everyone waited at home base. Fifteen minutes later, Sharon and Nate came walking from behind the building toward home base. They were smiling. We knew Nate had a crush on Sharon. We could tell they were probably kissing behind the building by the look on their faces.

LATCH-KEY KID

Like most of my friends, I was a latch-key kid. A latch-key kid let themselves in their homes after school. Every morning at 7:15 am, I caught the bus to Old Town Elementary School. After school, the bus dropped me back home to Everton Square around 3:00 pm. Calvin was supposed to be home by 4:00 pm to watch me until my mom got home.

When I got in from school, I fixed myself an afternoon snack, a bologna sandwich, cookies, and my favorite strawberry flavored Kool-Aid. I sat at the dining room table watching my favorite television shows, "Welcome Back Rod," "Starsky and Butch," and "The Jones."

Calvin was always late coming home. I finished my homework so I could go outside. Sometimes, I snooped around his bedroom when he was late coming home. He told me to stay out of his room, but I couldn't help myself. Calvin hid things in his room, and I wanted to see them. His bedroom door was closed. Checking his door to make sure it was unlocked; I slowly turned the door knob and tiptoed into his dark bedroom.

His blinds were closed, so I turned on the lamp that was on his nightstand. The room illuminated a dark shade of purple. Purple sheets draped over his headboard, and strobe lights hung from the ceiling of his room. A dashiki with bright colors hung over a chair, and posters of his favorite artists were taped on the walls.

I found incense laying on his dresser, so I lit it with the cigarette lighter. If my brother knew I was in his room, he would kill me. I heard Calvin knocking on the front door. "Boney, open the door. I forgot my key." I quickly turned off his lamp and blew out the incense. I yelled, "I'm coming!"

When I opened the door, Terry and Lonnie walked in behind Calvin. We greeted each other, then they followed Calvin to his room and closed the door. Calvin started playing one of his favorite albums, *Parliament Times*. He had a turntable and speakers in his bedroom. Calvin played his music loud enough for everyone in the building to hear. At times, he turned the music down to answer his phone.

I'd smell smoke coming from my brother's room. He and his buddies smoked something with a peculiar smell. Before my mom got home from work, Calvin's friends left the apartment. He knew my mom would be home by 6:00 pm. He locked the door when his friends left and threatened me. If I told my mom about what he and his friends had done, he'd beat me up.

I told him that he didn't scare me; I was going to tell mom. I was a tattletale. Calvin opened the balcony door to clear the smell coming from his bedroom; it didn't work. As soon as my mom walked through the door, she screamed, "Calvin! Were you smoking pot in my house?" He was busted. "Mom, it was Calvin, Terry, and Lonnie. They were smoking in Calvin's room!" I said.

If looks could kill, I would have been dead. He looked at me and balled his fists and placed one over his eye. That was his way of telling me he was going to beat me up for telling on him. Throughout the evening, he kept tripping me up when I walked past him in the living room. I'm glad he didn't hit me like he said he would.

The next day, on the ride home from school, a girl named Mena Jones threatened to beat me up. Mena moved to Lincoln City from New York. She was 12 years old and in the 6th grade. I was in the 5th grade. I didn't know how to fist fight. She told the kids on the bus she wanted to fight me, even though I hadn't said or done anything to her. Monique and Lexi said she told them I was "grittin" on her.

I sat in the back of the bus. Mena sat in the front of the bus. Afraid of fighting Mena, I planned to let everyone get off the bus first. Once the school bus approached Campbell Drive, my heart began beating fast. The bus pulled up to the stop in front of my apartment complex. Everyone got off the bus.

The boys on the bus were egging Mena on to hit me. They wanted to see a fight. I couldn't fight her in my school clothes. I had on a new skirt and shoes my mom bought me from Benny Shoes. Eventually, I got up from my seat and walked down the aisle of the school bus.

In one hand, I carried my violin. In the other hand, I had my school books. Lexi and Monique got off the bus first, and tried to talk Mena out of fighting me. They told her I hadn't been "grittin" on her. And I was scared to fight her. The only fight I had ever been in was with Deborah that time she called me the n-word.

I stepped off the bus and put my violin down on the ground because I didn't want anything to happen to it.

Mena yelled, "Do you wanna fight me?"

I asked her, "What are we fighting about?"

She said, "I saw you "grittin" on me on the bus."

I looked at her in shock because I knew I didn't grit on her. I remembered looking at her outfit when she got on the bus that morning, but that was it. With her fist balled, she started walking toward me. She was going to punch me. Before she hit me, I stood there not knowing if I should run or defend myself.

Making up an excuse to keep her from striking me, I came up with a plan of escape. I told her I had to take off my shoes, so she backed up. When I bent over to untie my shoelace, Mena turned her back while she waited. That's when I started running for my life. I grabbed my books and ran to my apartment building. Running away from Mena I yelled, "My brother, Calvin, is going to get you when he gets home!"

Running for my life, I practically flew up the steps to my building. Fumbling to put the key in the door, I gave up and started banging on the door. "Calvin! Calvin!" I yelled. "Mena said she is going to beat me up." He finally opened the door. "What? Hold on," he said. Calvin was mad.

I dropped my school books at the front door. Calvin and I walked back toward the bus stop to look for Mena, but she was gone. He walked around the complex calling her name. "Mena! Mena! Come out if you want to fight. You can fight me!" Mena was nowhere to be found.

Calvin asked a few of my classmates if they knew where she lived. I walked over to the bus stop to look for my violin. I accidentally left it at the bus stop before I ran from Mena. It was gone. How would I explain that I lost my violin? When Sharon and Lexi were headed to the ice cream truck, I asked them if they saw who took my violin.

Tears started rolling down my face, when I thought about how much money my mom would have to pay to replace my violin. Calvin and I walked back to the apartment. We gave up on finding Mena and my violin. I prayed my mom would understand that it wasn't my fault my violin was stolen. She walked through the door at her usual time.

"Eboni! Calvin! "I'm home!" she said.

Calvin was lying on the couch watching his favorite television show, *Milligan's Island*. Afraid to give her the bad news about my violin, I stayed in my room. She called me again, "Eboni, what are you doing?" I opened my door and came out to the living room to see what she wanted. "What's wrong?" she asked.

I explained that my violin was stolen because I had accidentally left it on the ground to avoid getting in a fight. "I laid my violin down on the street because a girl named Mena was going to be me up."Upset about the stolen violin, she sat down at the table.

I knew my mom couldn't afford to pay to replace the violin. Then, she told me she was glad I didn't fight. "I will call the music store tomorrow and tell them what happened, " she said. Then, she gave me a big hug. "Eboni. I'm glad you are okay," she said.

Determined to confront Mena the next morning, Calvin said he would walk me to the bus stop. I got on his nerves sometimes, but he protected me from anyone who wanted to harm me. And he could fight. He was the best big brother a sister could ever have.

On our way to the bus stop, I begged him not to beat Mena up because he could get in trouble for fighting a girl or go to jail. But he didn't care if he got in trouble. As we approached the bus stop, he asked me what Mena looked like. Calvin waited with me at the stop until the bus arrived, but we didn't see her.

He said, "If that girl Mena f***s with you again, tell her to meet me at the bus stop when you get off the bus." Mena didn't show up to the bus stop that morning. I got on the bus and sat up front near the bus driver. As the bus was pulling off, she came running up to the door.

The bus driver stopped so that she could get on. Mena walked right by me as if nothing happened. All the kids on the bus looked at me to see my reaction. I heard whispers and mumblings about what happened the day before, but I looked straight ahead to avoid eye contact with her. I didn't ever want to be accused of "grittin" on anyone again because I might end up getting in another fight.

3
REFLECTION

WANTING A FATHER

In elementary school, I barely weighed 80 pounds. I always compared myself to the other girls in my class. My mother said I inherited the pug-like nose from the Lee family, and I hated it. I especially hated being dark skinned. I didn't know what my father looked like, but he must have been dark skinned like me.

Saturday was my favorite day of the week, but I had to do chores. Before I started my chores, I watched my favorite TV shows first. I laid on the couch in my pajamas with a box of cereal and had a glass of grape Kool-Aid on the coffee table. *Good Vibes*, my favorite television show, was on every morning.

Good Vibes was about an African American family who lived in the ghetto. The father always complimented his daughter. He told her how pretty and smart she was. In one episode, the father comforted his daughter after she broke up with her boyfriend. He reminded her that she was beautiful, even if the boy didn't see it.

Watching this episode made me wish I had a father like that. No man had ever told me I was beautiful. One day, I hoped my father would tell me I was beautiful like the father did to his daughter on *Good Vibes*. He'd always dote on his daughter on the show. Sometimes he'd bring her flowers to remind her that he loved her.

I heard my mom open her bedroom door, so I jumped up off the couch before she fussed at me about my chores. The number one rule of the house was that I had to do finish my chores before watching TV. She knew I hadn't finished cleaning my room and the bathroom. I turned off the TV and started cleaning up.

After I finished, I watched several episodes of *Good Vibes*. By that time, it's almost midnight. The National Anthem started playing, then

53

the fuzzy gray screen appeared. It was time for me to go to bed, so I got up and turned the knob to power off the television.

My mom deserved the parent of the year award. She filled many roles for Calvin and me: mother, father, provider, confidant, and protector. She tried to instill in us the importance of being good and kind to everyone and to each other. We may not have had all the toys and gadgets we wanted, but she gave us a lot of love. Love was more important than things.

CAN I HAVE A CHANCE?

Old Town Elementary selected me to be a safety patrol officer because I had "very good" in every class on my report card. The safety patrol officers wore a bright orange colored band. The band crossed the front of my body, hooked around my waist, and fastened in the front with a silver buckle. I wore my patrol belt over my coat or my clothes, depending on the weather.

Every morning, patrol duty started as soon as I got to the bus stop. As a patrol officer, my duty was to make sure students remained safe on and off the school bus. Students also had to behave in an orderly manner. One perk of being a safety patrol officer was being in charge of my peers. I stood in the aisle of the bus to maintain order, ensuring the other kids followed the rules.

There were a few cute boys on my bus: Stan, Darren, and Michael. I had a crush on them. They were in Mrs. Hollaman's class. I really liked Stan. He was tall, and he had caramel-colored skin, nice teeth, and dimples. Darren was my height and had a medium brown complexion.

Michael was tall and light skinned, with freckles. He was an athlete and the best basketball player in the complex and at Old Town Elementary. Sometimes the boys teased me. They "joanned" on me by calling me out of my name. It hurt my feelings when they called me "ugly," "skinny," and "darkie." I still liked them, even though they made me cry inside.

One day, I wore a new outfit my mom bought me from Sears Style. It was a red and white jumpsuit with a zipper in the front. My hair was pressed and curled in the mushroom hairstyle. The curls were long and almost passed my shoulders. I felt pretty that day. While waiting at the bus stop, Stan told me I looked pretty. He said he liked my outfit and hair. I blushed. Stan made my day. I was on cloud nine.

Walking into the classroom, Mrs. Hollaman always stood at her door to greet us. She was my favorite teacher, and I was one of her favorite students. Mrs. Hollaman always smiled and seemed happy to see us. She was a Caucasian woman with long, black hair, and she wore funny-looking glasses.

Every morning, Mrs. Hollaman gave us free time after we said the Pledge of Allegiance. It lasted for 15 minutes. During free time, no one was allowed to talk. Students could read a book, color, or do something fun while remaining quiet. I liked to draw pictures of flowers.

Drawing in my workbook, I looked up and noticed Stan was staring at me. Smiling, he started writing on a piece of paper. After he wrote on the paper, he folded it up and passed it to one of our classmates. I wondered if Stan was going to ask me for a chance. A "chance" is a note written by a boy to ask a girl to be his girlfriend. The boy writes the note and sends it to the girl, asking for a chance.

The note is sent through one of his friends in the classroom or on the school bus. The note might say, "Will you go with me?" or "Can I have a chance?" When the girl received the note, she responded by checking "yes" or "no." Then she passed it back to the boy who asked her.

Earlier that morning, Stan had complimented my hair and outfit. I saw his note being passed around the classroom to my other classmates. Free time was a perfect time to pass it because Mrs. Hollaman sat at her desk grading papers. She didn't notice what we were doing.

Although, if she caught us, she would take it and read it to the entire class. That was embarrassing. I watched Stan's note being passed from his side of the room, to Darren in the second row, then to the third row to Michael. I hoped he was sending the note to me.

I sat on the third row towards the middle, and saw the note being passed in my direction. Excited, about receiving Stan's note, I kept looking up at Mrs. Hollaman to make sure the coast was clear. She was still focused on her work, grading papers. Michael passed the note to Sherri.

Next, the note would come to me because Sherri sat beside me. She gave me the note. It had my name written on it. I placed the note in my lap. The note was folded up 7 times. I opened it. My heart started beating fast, then it was the moment I had been waiting for. I wondered if Stan was going to ask me for a chance.

When I opened the note, it said, "Eboni. Do you have an extra pencil

I can borrow?" My heart dropped with disappointment. Stan was staring at me, waiting for my response. I nodded my head to show that I would lend him a pencil. Why didn't he ask Sherri or one of the other girls sitting in his row? I pulled an extra pencil out of my desk. Then, Stan raised his hand to ask Mrs. Hollaman if he could get up from his desk to get a pencil.

THE DAY CALVIN LEFT HOME

It was a sad and dark day on September 12, 1976. I got home from school at my normal time. I hadn't eaten lunch at school, so I was hungry. My after-school snack was a bologna sandwich and a glass of grape Kool-Aid. Calvin was in the kitchen washing the dishes.

"Hey, Calvin!" I said. He didn't respond. "Calvin, what's wrong with you, boy?" Still no response. Something must have been wrong. Calvin would never let me get away with calling him a boy.

Someone began knocking on the door, but Calvin kept washing the dishes. I walked to the door and answered it. I yelled, "Who is it? Just a minute." Then, I looked through the peephole. Two white men dressed in dark blue uniforms were at the door. It was the police.

One of the officers asked, "Does Calvin Davis live here?" I said, "Yes." They asked if they could come in, so I opened the door. Calvin had gone into his bedroom. I called him. Then, the police officer said, "Calvin Davis we need to speak with you." The police stood waiting in the living room.

I went to my mom's bedroom to call her, hoping she would be at work. With his head down, Calvin came out of his bedroom and walked into the living room. By the time I walked out of my mom's room, I heard the police put handcuffs on Calvin. They escorted him out of the apartment. The officers took him out to their car in handcuffs. He looked back at me to say goodbye.

I followed the police and Calvin down the steps. The officers put Calvin in the backseat of their dark gray police car. When they pulled off, I walked up the steps back into the apartment. I went straight to my bedroom and cried my eyes out for my brother. He was gone.

My mom arrived home from work around 7:00 pm. I could tell she had gotten the bad news about Calvin. Her eyes were puffy and bloodshot red, as if she had been crying. She walked straight to her bedroom and closed the door. I sat in front of her bedroom door. Every time the phone rang, she cried explaining what happened to Calvin. The phone rang nonstop.

Listening to my mother through the bedroom door, it seemed as though Calvin was innocent. He was with a group of boys at the basketball court when a white boy was shot. My mom kept saying that Calvin didn't kill the white boy and that he was only there when it happened.

He was guilty by association. My mom had warned Calvin about hanging out with those bad boys. They were known around town for always being trouble with the police. At that time, Lincoln City was predominantly white, so young black boys were incarcerated, convicted, and falsely accused of committing crimes.

Days went by, and Calvin didn't come home. My mom cried every night. I wondered if my brother was ever coming back home. I couldn't stop thinking about him. Late one Friday afternoon, around 5:00 pm, my mom came home early from work. She told me to get dressed so that we could visit Calvin at the jail.

En route to the jail, my mom drove fast because she was anxious to see him. It was the first time she was able to see him since he was arrested. Walking through the front door of the jail, we were greeted by the prison guards. They asked for our names, then searched for us on the visitor's list. Then, they asked us for the name of the inmate we were visiting.

After we gave them Calvin's name, the guards directed us to another area where we were frisked. We had to put our arms up and get patted down. Then, the guards looked through my mom's purse. After we finished going through security, a guard escorted us to the visitor waiting area. The waiting room had no chairs; it was standing-room only.

The room was full of African American families. The guard called our name, so we followed him down the hall to another room. There was one row with 6 phone booths, and each one was separated by glass. Calvin walked up to the glass to see us. My mom and I moved closer to the glass to speak to him.

Calvin had on an orange long-sleeve jumpsuit. Tears started rolling from my eyes. My mom wanted to touch Calvin's hand. Placing her hand on the glass window, she picked up the black phone. Then, Calvin picked up his phone. When mom asked Calvin if he was okay, he looked down and didn't respond.

Lost for words, he could barely talk. I asked my mom if I could talk to him, so she handed me the phone. I asked my brother when he was coming home, but he said he didn't know. Calvin wiped the tears from his eyes with his sleeve. Once he started crying, I couldn't help but cry as well.

I missed my brother and wanted him home. My mom couldn't bear seeing Calvin behind the glass window in the jail. After a few minutes, she told him we had to leave. Placing her hand on the glass as if to touch Calvin, she told him goodbye. We both waved our goodbyes.

Days and months passed; Calvin was still at the Lincoln City Jail. Our apartment was quiet without him. There was no more loud music, smell of incense, snooping in his room, or visits from his buddies. I missed my brother. Thinking about him made me sad.

AUDITION DAY

At 13 years old, I started growing and developing into a young woman. My mom purchased training bras from Zaire's Value Department Store off of Millerton Pike. I was a late bloomer compared to the rest of the girls in my class. They already wore bras, had perms in their hair, and wore makeup.

Being able to finally wear a training bra made me fit in with my friends, but I still hated the way I looked. From my complexion, to my height and nappy hair, I felt out of place. I was envious of the girls who had straight long hair. My hair never grew past my shoulders. I wanted to be tall and pretty like the other girls.

Rose Green Middle School was just a few miles down the street from my apartment. The bumpy and crazy ride to school with my friends on the school bus was a lot of fun. No longer on patrol duty, I sat next to my friends on the bus every day. Sometimes, the bus driver threatened to pull the bus over if we didn't settle down. The boys were rowdy and out of control in the back of the bus. They told yo mamma jokes.

Keith started "bustin people out" or making fun of other kids as soon as he got on the bus. "James, yo mamma so ugly, fat, and dirty, when she looked in the mirror, she broke it in to pieces!" The entire bus burst into laughter. If you laughed too loud, the boys would "joan" on you.

I looked forward to going to school every day to see the cute boys at Rose Green. Most of them liked my girlfriends. They didn't look at me because I was too dark. During gym class, one of my friends asked me to put my arm next to hers to show how much darker I was than her. I tried to avoid being in the sun, especially during the summer.

But I couldn't help being dark. I loved going to the pool and playing outside with my friends. My family constantly reminded me to stay out of the sun to keep from getting blacker, as if being too black wasn't good. I didn't like the complexion God gave me but what was I to do?

In October 1978, I auditioned for the Rose Green Middle School pom-pom team. The pom-pom team performed during halftime at the school's basketball games. Our school mascot was a jaguar. If I made the team, the cute purple and white uniform would make me stand out. Being a member of the pom-pom team, would help make the guys notice me.

The team's uniform included a dark purple pleated skirt, white turtle-neck, and a purple and white vest. During the first week of school, Ms. Johnson, the pom-pom team advisor, posted a flyer that said the auditions were on October 2nd in the cafeteria. If I made the team, the boys would surely notice me. That would make me so happy.

The Saturday morning before the audition, I watched back-to-back episodes of *Soul Main*. *Soul Main* had the best dancers in the world. When Don Covington, the host, announced the *Soul Main Line*, I stood by the TV ready to take lessons from the dancers on the show. I mimicked their dance moves. They did the robot, the bump, and the funky chicken.

In between the episodes, I played my 45s, or records, on the turntable in the dining room. The turntable was a light brown rectangular-shaped machine that looked like a box. My mom bought me a few of my favorite albums and 45s by Michael Jams, Minnie Ripper, Rapper's Choice, Nancy True, and the Isley Quartet.

On October 2nd, my special day, I auditioned for the team. Without any formal dance training, I tried out for the pom-pom team. I had rhythm and picked up a few dance moves from *Soul Main*. I knew my fancy moves would surely earn me a spot on the pom-pom team.

My cousin had pressed and curled my hair into my favorite hairstyle, the mushroom. It was a popular hairstyle at school. My hair was straight all over and the curls tucked under all around my head. The shape of the hairstyle looked just like a mushroom. Most of the girls at school wore their hair in that style.

The bell rang, signaling the end of the last period of the school day. After I left my gym class, I got dressed for the audition. I wore my gym shoes and a cute bright red t-shirt and matching red shorts. I was nervous. I had prayed the night before and asked God to help me make the team. I prepared a dance routine I learned watching Soul Main.

Thirty girls lined up in the cafeteria to try out for the team, but there were only 15 slots. Everyone lined up to get their numbers; I got number seven. After everyone received their numbers, Ms. Johnson put on Michael Jam's "ABC song." I loved that song. Then, she told us to start dancing to the music. I danced just like Michael Jams. Snapping my fingers and dancing from side to side, I did all his famous dance moves.

At the end of the song, I went straight into a split. Then, Ms. Johnson placed us in two lines. She stood up front and taught us a pom-pom routine. We followed her every move. The routine consisted of high kicks, turns, and marches. At the end of the audition, Ms. Johnson told us she would post the list of the girls who made the team on the bulletin board by the main office.

On Friday morning, as soon as I got off the bus, I walked to the office to look at the bulletin board. Mine was the third name on the list. I made the team! I screamed, "I made the RGM pom-pom team!" My classmates in the hallway smiled as they walked by. Some of them congratulated me. I ran to my locker to tell my friends. I couldn't wait to tell my mom I had earned a spot on the team. Thanks to lucky number seven.

FIRST KISS

Making the pom-pom team gave me a boost of confidence. I finally fit in with my peers. The attention from the boys made me feel good about myself because they started looking at me differently. There was one boy I liked. His name was Derrick. I had known Derrick since Old Town Elementary School.

A few weeks prior to making the pom-pom team, I saw Derrick in the cafeteria. I spoke to him in the hallway, but he didn't respond. In between classes, I purposely walked by his locker pretending to look for one of my girlfriends on the team. I prayed that he would talk to me. If he did, I would be the happiest girl in the world.

Back in the day, Derrick used to tease me by calling me names like the other kids. When I told my mom how the boys used to tease me, she said that boys usually teased girls they liked. Derrick didn't "crack" on me like he did the other girls. When a boy "cracked" on a girl, it meant he wanted to talk to her and asked for her phone number.

On Friday, December 3, 1978, I made my debut on the pom-pom team. That morning, when I got off the school bus, I walked into the building to show off my pom-pom uniform. I intentionally walked by Derrick's locker so that he could see me in my uniform. Ms. Johnson told us we could wear our pom-pom uniforms to school that day.

Switching my hips in my short skirt as I walked towards Derrick's locker, I hoped he would notice me. Standing by his locker, he looked over at me and greeted me. I almost fainted. In shock that he spoke to me, I smiled and started walking to class. I didn't expect him to speak to me. He made my day.

The basketball game was right after lunch at 1:00pm. Ms. Johnson made an announcement over the intercom asking teachers to release all members of the pom-pom team to the cafeteria after 5th period. I was excited and ready to perform. I couldn't wait to show off my dance routine and pom-pom moves with the team.

Dressed in my uniform, holding my purple and white pom-poms, I couldn't wait to perform. Ms. Johnson choreographed a special Christmas pom-pom routine, which consisted of synchronized arm motions showing off our purple and white pom-poms. We danced to Michael Jam's "Frosty the Snowman."

After everyone lined up in the cafeteria, Ms. Johnson escorted us to the gym to get ready to perform. I had butterflies in my stomach and was a nervous wreck. The team marched in the gym waving our pom-poms from side to side. The captain blew her whistle three times, then the music began. Our routine began with a high march. We lifted our legs high like soldiers, then we danced.

As soon as we started our dance routine, everyone stood up singing, clapping, and dancing to the music. At the end of our routine, the captain blew her whistle three times, then we marched back to the cafeteria. The basketball players, teachers, and my classmates loved our dance routine. We got a standing ovation. Ms. Johnson told us we were outstanding. She slapped our hands up high in the air as we walked back to the cafeteria.

I left the cafeteria and started walking back to my locker to get my books. Derrick was there waiting for me. "Eboni, you got some smooth dance moves," he said. I blushed. I couldn't believe he was paying attention to me. "Thank you, Derrick," I said. I opened my locker to get my books.

I freaked out when Derrick started moving closer to me. My heart almost jumped out of my chest because I didn't know what he was about to do. I looked up, and he put his hand on my cheek to turn my face towards his. I looked around to see if anyone was in the hallway. No one was around.

Suddenly, he pulled me close to him. I felt my heart was beating faster. His hazel brown eyes had me in a trance as he leaned in to kiss me. Then, his soft lips touched mine. He showed me how to tongue kiss him back, and it felt good. It was mushy and it gave me goosebumps. I had never tongue kissed a boy before.

I opened my eyes after Derrick passionately kissed me. I was at a loss for words that someone as cute as him would pick me of all the girls on the team. I never thought he, or any of the boys, would ever notice me. Coming out of a daze from his kiss, I asked him if I could call him when I got home from school.

Ms. Johnson gave each member of the pom-pom team a hall pass, in case we were late to class. Walking down the hallway, she saw me standing by my locker. "Eboni, aren't you supposed to be on your way to class?" she asked. "Yes, Ms. Johnson," I replied. I quickly wrote Derrick's phone number on a small piece of paper. "I will call you tonight," I said.

I couldn't believe he finally noticed me. God had answered my prayers. I felt like the luckiest girl in the world. After I finished my homework, I laid on the floor in the living room. I called Derrick using the beige kitchen phone, stretching the cord into the living room.

Around 9:00 pm, I heard my mom put the key in the door. She was home, so I rushed to get off the phone. That night, I laid in my bed daydreaming about Derrick and our first kiss. I kept replaying our first kiss in my head from the minute he walked up to me until his lips met mine. I looked forward to seeing him at school tomorrow so that we could do it all over again.

CONVERSION TO THE MORMON FAITH

My mom and I hadn't gone to Mt. Lebanon Baptist Church with Mamma G in a while. She worked overtime on Sundays, but she was off the 1st Sunday of each month. Before we went to church, my mom played music on the local gospel radio station. Some of her favorite gospel artists were James C., Walter Hampton, Mahailia Janton, and Aretha Franks. Her favorite song was "Take My Hand, Lord" by Mahalia Janton.

One Saturday evening, there was a knock on our apartment door around 6:00 pm. I ran to the door and looked through the peephole. I saw two young white guys smiling. Both dressed in a white shirt, tie, and black slacks, they stood waiting for me to open the door.

"Who is it?" I asked.

"We are the missionaries," they responded in unison. I opened the door. They both had a Bible in their hand.

Asking if they could come in to talk to us, I said, "Hold on." I told my mom that missionaries were at the door. She came to the door with a puzzled look on her face. No church missionary had ever knocked on our door before. They seemed friendly and polite.

One of them spoke and said, "Hello, my name is Elder J. from the Church of Jesus Christ of Latter-day Saints. Can we come in for a few minutes to talk about the Gospel of Jesus Christ?" They promised it would only take a few minutes of our time. My mom agreed that they could come into our home.

The missionaries told us they spent two years of their lives, knocking on doors and sharing the Gospel of Jesus Christ and the Book of Mormon. When they came in, my mom told me to turn off the TV. Annoyed by the timing of their visit, I missed one of my favorite TV shows. They pulled out a Bible and another book with lots of pictures. I couldn't wait until they left so I could finish watching my shows.

Intrigued by the Book of Mormon, my mom listened intently to the missionaries' presentation about their modern-day prophet, Joseph Smith. They prayed with us before they left and asked if they could come back next week. My mom said they could, so they scheduled the next visit. She seemed curious about their faith.

After the missionaries left, my mom said, "There was something special about those guys. I want to know more about Mormons." She had only heard of one black person in the church. Her friends told her they were a cult. My mother had a lot of questions to ask them when they came back for another lesson.

The following week, the missionaries came back and shared another lesson from the Bible and the Book of Mormon. The Book of Mormon was smaller than the Bible; it had a navy-blue cover and lots of pictures inside. The missionaries made my mom feel comfortable sharing her feelings about religion and God.

By the sixth visit, they asked my mom if she wanted to be baptized and join the church. After pondering and praying about what the missionaries shared with her, my mom converted to the Mormon faith. She asked me if I wanted to convert, too. In order to convert to the Mormon faith, my mom and I had to be baptized all over again.

On a Saturday afternoon in 1978, we got baptized into the Mormon faith. My mom picked up Mamma G to attend the ceremony. She didn't seem happy about our conversion to another faith. We knew Mamma G would never leave Mt. Lebanon Baptist Church, but she was there to support us. We loved her for coming out to see us get baptized.

The day before the baptism, the missionaries instructed us to wear all white to church. Before the baptism began, we sat in the sanctuary waiting with the missionaries, Bishop Parks, Mamma G, and a few members of the church. Once the baptismal pool was filled, everyone was directed to enter the room.

We walked in with Elder J. and Elder Osborne; they wore all white. Elder J. opened up the baptism service with a prayer. After the prayer, Bishop Parks explained the importance of being baptized. The Bishop said,

"In the Bible, the book of Acts, chapter 2, verse 38, Peter replied, 'Repent and be baptized, every one of you, in the name of Jesus Christ for the forgiveness of your sins. And you will receive the gift of the Holy Spirit.'"

After the bishop read the scripture, Elder Osborne asked my mom to enter the baptismal font. The font looked like a big tub of water with white walls; it was at least four feet deep. Everyone else watched as she walked down the steps into the pool of water where Elder Osbourne was standing and waiting. He reached out his hand to help her.

After the prayer of baptism, Elder Osborne held my mom, then dipped her in the pool of water. She came up smiling after the elder baptized her. The sisters of the church helped her walk up the steps, waiting with towels in their hands. They escorted her to the lady's bathroom to dry off and get dressed.

I was next. Elder Osbourne called me over to the baptismal font. I walked down the steps to meet him. He prayed the baptismal prayer for me and immersed me in the water. A couple of teenage girls waited for me with towels and helped me out of the pool of water. They walked with me to the bathroom to help me get dressed.

Afterwards, everyone walked down the hallway to another meeting room. Mamma G was already there waiting for us. The sisters of the church escorted my mom and me to the room after we got dressed. Mamma G was seated in the back row. Bishop Parks explained the Gift of the Holy Ghost to everyone in the room.

Receiving the Gift of the Holy Ghost, was next. The bishop called both Elder J. and Elder Osbourne to the front of the room. An empty chair was placed in front of the room. Bishop Parks said, "Sister Davis can you please come to the front of the room? My mom walked to the front and sat in the chair.

The bishop and the missionaries formed a circle around her, laying the palms of their hands on her head. The bishop prayed over my mom and she received the Gift of the Holy Ghost. She smiled when they finished. They told her she could be seated on a row up front.

Next, Bishop Parks signaled for me to come up front and sit in the chair. The bishop and the missionaries formed a circle around me, laying their hands on my head. Elder J. prayed over me to receive the gift of the

Holy Ghost. Afterwards, they told me I could sit beside my mom. It was a memorable and joyous occasion.

After the ceremony was over, we were officially members of the Mormon church. The bishop, missionaries, and sisters of the church greeted us and welcomed us into the Everton Ward. They invited everyone to a small reception in the fellowship hall. We ate cookies and drank punch. A few of the members had come over to welcome us and shake our hands.

On Sunday, we attended the Everton Ward for the first time. Walking into the sanctuary, my mom and I noticed we were the only African Americans in the building. All eyes were on us as if we were foreigners in a new land. We felt the stares and glares from members as we sat down in the sanctuary. I wondered if some members had never seen black people before.

The stares made me feel a little uncomfortable. I couldn't discern if they were staring because they knew us or because we were black. A couple of people came over to greet us, shook our hands, and welcomed us into Everton Ward. Some continued to stare. Before the service began, Bishop Parks asked us to stand, and he acknowledged us as new members of the church.

Learning about my new faith, I discovered the church service was different from Mt. Lebanon. The service was three hours long. The first hour was called the sacrament, the second hour was Sunday School, and the last hour was Relief Society for the women. The Young Women was designed for girls ages 12 to 18 years old.

Instead of a pastor, a bishop presided over the church meeting. The missionaries were seated on the first two rows of the church to serve the sacrament, which was communion at Mt. Lebanon. At Everton Ward, communion was taken every Sunday. The sacrament is a piece of bread, which represented the body of Jesus Christ; the water represented his blood.

It wasn't as tasty as the communion at Mt. Lebanon; I missed the red juice and the piece of cracker. During the sacrament, everyone in the sanctuary remained quiet. There was no mass choir or sanctuary choir to sing songs. There were no solos, choirs marching down the aisles, or swaying to music. The service was different; it wasn't what I expected.

Bishop Parks asked everyone to open up their hymn books to begin the service. After sacrament, one of the members walked to the front of the church to give a talk from the Bible and the Book of Mormon. I never saw one offering plate passed the entire time during service. How did they collect tithes and offerings for the church? Mt. Lebanon passed the offering plate at least three times to collect tithes and offerings from its members.

I missed hearing gospel music, the sanctuary choir, and listening to the organ at Mt. Lebanon. There were no more sanctified sisters shouting "hallelujah" and "thank you, Lord." Before we went to Sunday School, the bishop encouraged everyone to keep the Sabbath day holy, which meant no television, shopping, or any recreational activities. My mom said I couldn't watch television or play outside to keep the Sabbath day holy.

During that time, being a black Mormon was almost unheard of. One of the reasons why some blacks didn't join the church was because blacks couldn't hold the priesthood. The priesthood is the authority to act in the name of God; only men in the church had this authority. I never asked the missionaries why black people couldn't hold the priesthood. For years, my mom and I were the only blacks at Everton Ward.

There were a few black Mormons in other wards, but not very many. What I liked most about the Mormons was their sense of family. Every member of the church was important and considered family. The bishop told my mom she could call him or his wife whenever she needed them. He told her that he or his wife would be available if she wanted to talk or needed help.

A couple of weeks later, my mom reached out to Bishop Parks. One early morning, around 7:00 am, her car wouldn't start. She called Bishop Parks. "Good morning, Bishop Parks. My car won't start. Can you give me a jump?" she asked.

He answered, "Sure, Sister Davis. I'll be right over. What is your address?"

My mom was relieved Bishop Parks was on his way to help her. He arrived within 30 minutes, then knocked on our apartment door. "Hello Eboni. How are you? I'm here to help your mom. Tell her I'm outside. I'm happy to help her start her car." Bishop Parks seemed happy and unbothered about having to come out so early in the morning.

My mom ran out outside with her purse to meet him. I looked out the window and saw Bishop Parks jump start her car within 5 minutes. She handed him some money, but he refused it. He shook her hand, waved goodbye, and walked to his car. Then, my mom pulled out of her parking space and went to work.

At times, I was embarrassed to tell my friends I was a Mormon. They probably thought I was crazy. I avoided conversations about religion because my friends didn't have anything good to say about Mormons. Most of them said that they didn't like black people. It was hard convincing them that Mormons were good people and that the church wasn't a cult. It didn't matter. I was content with being a member and I enjoyed my new friends and the families I met.

4
FINDING MYSELF

CAMPING: A FIRST

Every week, the sisters of the church sponsored activities for the young women of the church. We met every Wednesday night. I enjoyed meeting my new friends at church. The young women in my group were 13 years old like me. Some of the activities included cooking lessons, skiing, and camping. I looked forward to participating in everything, except camping.

The annual young women camping trip was in June. I didn't want to sleep in a tent and fight off any bugs. It didn't sound like fun to me. The sisters in the church and my mother wanted me to sign up. My mom was standing beside me and agreed with Sister Lee that I should go.

It took a few weeks for Sister Lee and my new friends to convince me to go to camp. Eventually, I signed up after our meeting on Wednesday night. I thought it might be fun camping out with my new friends. They talked me into going and promised me I wouldn't regret it. The girls said they had fun last year.

On June 20th, we boarded a school bus to go to camp. Twenty girls piled on the bus with our sleeping bags, tents, backpacks, coolers full of food and drinks, and other camping equipment. The ride to the campsite was two hours long. We sang songs and laughed on our way there. When we arrived at the site, I immediately had second thoughts about my decision.

There were so many tall trees, dirt roads, and bugs; there was no sign of shelter. The bees were buzzing around my head and I didn't want to get stung. Flies were everywhere, and they were getting on my nerves. The girls and I sprayed down our legs and arms to fight off the bugs. It didn't work. I wanted to be inside, not outdoors.

I wondered how I was going to get a good night's rest while sleeping on the ground. Eating food cooked by campfire wasn't going to taste good.

What a nightmare! I had changed my mind and wanted to go back home. But it was too late.

The first day of camp was a total disaster. It was a scorching 90 degrees outside, so I perspired profusely. I didn't like the heat. Cammi and Lynn said they would set up our tent. I couldn't stand the heat, so I stood by and watched while they worked. Up to four girls could fit in the tent; there were three of us.

Cammi came from a family of six. She'd been a member of the church since she was born. Lynn joined the church with her mom last year. They seemed intrigued by me being the only black girl at camp. Standing outside in the heat made me thirsty and hungry, so I was glad when Sister Lee said she was going to fix lunch.

We put our backpacks and camping gear in our tent. Sister Fair said we would do crafts after lunch. I loved arts and crafts. Sister Lee fixed soup she had made from scratch over the campfire. The soup was tasty, but it wasn't like a real home-cooked meal. I didn't care; I was hungry.

After lunch, we gathered around a brown wooden bench to start our craft project. The project was carving a picture on a piece of wood. I selected a picture of Raggedy Ann and Andy. Sister Fair showed everyone how to use the carving tools. I had never carved wood before. She told everyone to be careful because the tools were very sharp.

Before we started carving, we traced our images onto the wood. I had a difficult time seeing the image after I traced it, so I did it again. Sister Fair told us to keep the wood flat on the table. I didn't follow her instructions. Holding the piece of wood in my hand, I cut right into the palm of my left hand.

I screamed, "Help!" Blood gushed out all over my clothes. I yelled out to Sister Fair. "Can you help me? I cut myself!"

She jumped up from the bench and ran to get the first aid kit from her tent. When she returned, she took out a piece of white gauze and began applying pressure to stop the blood from gushing out. The gash was about two inches long. She thought I might need stitches.

She continued to apply pressure; eventually, the bleeding stopped. Sister Fair cleaned my wound with peroxide and wrapped it up tight with gauze. Then, told me to change my gauze every hour. What a way to start my first day of camp. I hoped the rest of the week would be better.

On the second day of camp, I had my first hiking experience. After breakfast, I walked over to the small gray building with my wash cloth, toothbrush, and soap to take a shower. The building, small with hardly any light coming through the windows, had spiders and bugs crawling all over the shower walls. I placed my things on the small black bench to take a shower.

That's when I saw something crawling. I screamed! Cammi and Lynn came running to the building to find out what happened. I told them there was something crawling in my shower stall. They looked around to see if they could find anything. I asked them to stay with me until I got out of the shower. I brushed my teeth instead, fearing something was going to crawl on me.

Later, we all gathered around to prepare for our morning hike. Sister Lee and Sister Fair told everyone to wear comfortable clothes and shoes. I wore shorts and a t-shirt. I didn't have any hiking boots, so I wore my tennis shoes. We packed our snacks in small brown paper bags.

Cammi, Lynn, and another girl, Samantha, and I decided to walk together on the hike. We sang, laughed, and had a lot of fun hiking on the trails for about an hour. I was exhausted and my feet were hurting. The hike made me hungry; I was ready for lunch. My stomach was growling.

The sisters gave us free time to relax in our tents after the hike. We laid around until it was time to eat. Before sunset, we sat in a circle around the campfire to roast marshmallows. We went to bed around 9:00 pm. A few of the girls wanted to play practical jokes after the sisters went to sleep. I laid in the tent listening to the other girls laughing and giggling as they wrapped our tent with toilet paper.

Cammi said, "Who's out there?"

The girls laughed and said "Shhhhh." Cammi and Lynn said they recognized the girls' voices.

Through the tent, I could see the bright lights from their flashlights. I heard them as they walked over to other tents. We laughed when they left. I eventually fell off to sleep.

By the third day of camp, I was ready to go home. Camping wasn't for me, especially because I was the only African American girl there. I had my share of awkward moments when some of the girls stared at me.

Cammi and Lynn said they had black friends at school, but the other girls appeared to have never seen a black person before.

On the last day of camp, the leaders said we could go to the pool. I was glad it was the last day of camp. I didn't care if my hair got wet because I had a perm. Splashing water on each other in the pool, Cammi, Lynn, and I had a lot of fun. We competed with each other swimming from one end of the pool to the other. We swam a few laps. They seemed surprised that I knew how to swim, especially after I jumped in the deep end of the pool.

They looked confused. I had a hunch that although they had black friends at school, they didn't interact with them much. The lifeguard blew his whistle for a break.

Lynn asked me, "Eboni, can I feel your hair?"

I didn't know why she wanted to feel my hair. "Sure!" I said.

Then, I asked, "Lynn, why are you curious about my hair?"

She responded, "I've never felt a black person's hair before."

Being the only black girl at camp, I was the odd ball in the group. Gently touching my hair, she asked if I ever wore cornrows. I told her I did sometimes during the summer months. "How do you do your hair like that?" she inquired. I told her I wished I had hair like hers. The girls had all shades and textures of hair from blonde to dark brown, short to long, and curly to straight.

Lynn asked me if I could braid her hair. Her hair was too straight and stringy. I smiled and told her I would try. It was puzzling how my new friends wanted to know more about my hair and culture. At times it felt awkward and sometimes I felt offended. Why did they want their hair to be like mine?

On the last night of camp, Lynn, Cammi, and I stayed up late talking about boys at our schools. The sisters stopped by everyone's tent to remind us to pack up our belongings because we would be leaving camp around 7:00 am. Morning came, and it was time to get up and go home. I helped Cammi and Lynn take down the tent. I couldn't wait to get home and shower in my own bathroom.

Everyone piled on the school bus to head back to the Everton Ward building. Most of the girls slept the entire ride home. When the bus pulled into the parking lot of the church, my mom stood waiting for me. She gave me a big hug, told me she had missed me, and said I looked like I had gotten a tan.

On our way to the apartment, I could tell I needed to shower and brush my teeth as soon as I walked through the door. That's what I did. I took a shower and laid down in my comfy bed. Going to youth camp with the church was my first and last time ever. The highlight of my adventure was swimming on the last night of camp. I chalked it up as an experience I would never forget.

PLAYING BASKETBALL

Sister Little, one of the sisters in the ward, formed a Young Women basketball team. She asked all the young women if they wanted to join the team. During our Young Women meeting on Wednesday night, she asked if I had ever played basketball. I told her I hadn't, but I was willing to try.

Sister Little seemed like a nice lady. She told us she used to play basketball in college. Promising she would teach everyone how to play, I agreed to sign up. At first, playing basketball seemed like a bad idea because I didn't want to break my nails. Running up and down the court and getting sweaty like the boys wasn't appealing to me.

Every Saturday morning, the basketball team practiced from 8:00 am until 9:00 am. That seemed too early to go to practice. There were eight girls on the team. Sister Little taught us how to do lay-ups, bounce and pass the basketball, and shoot. I had fun at practice with my new friends on the team.

After a few weeks of practice, I started doing layups, free throws, and dribbling the basketball. My teammates and Sister Little gave me the nickname "Ebbi." I felt a little awkward being the only black girl on the team, so I focused on having fun instead. I wanted to learn how to play. If I got really good, I could try out for the team at my school.

By the time we started playing against other teams in the other wards, I had developed into a pretty good basketball player. Our first game was a scrimmage against the Blue Plains Ward Young Women's team. The Blue Plains Ward was on the other side of Lincoln City. They had the same number of girls on their team. Watching them warm up before the game, they looked taller and more experienced.

The girls on the Blue Plains team tried to intimidate me by bouncing their balls around me when I warmed up. I think they wanted to see if I could really play basketball or if I was new to the game. I faked like I didn't know how to shoot the ball. They kept watching me to see if I made any of my free throw shots.

When the scrimmage started, Blue Plains' defense was all over me, blocking me from shooting the ball and scoring. Most whites felt all blacks were good at playing sports. Little did they know that it was my first time playing. I remembered everything Sister Little taught me about how to dribble the ball. They couldn't figure me out.

For the first half of the game, Sister Little put me in as guard. At halftime, the score was tied 8 to 8. The crowd cheered for both teams. The score was close until the last five minutes of the game. Cammi came in as guard for the second half of the game, and I was the center. There were two minutes left in the game, and the score was still tied.

Cammi dribbled down the court and passed the ball to Lynn. I was in the center waiting for Lynn to pass the ball to me so that I could drive the ball down the center of the court to score. With 30 seconds left on the scoreboard, Lynn finally passed me the ball, and I drove the ball down the court to score. The score became 10 to 8; we were winning.

The Blue Plains team had the ball and tried to pass it to one of their players. Cammi jumped in front of the player and caught the ball. She passed the ball to me, and I shot the ball by the free throw line and scored. We won our first game with a score of 12 to 8.

Sister Little jumped up and down on the sidelines; she was so happy we won the game. Celebrating our first win, we all went out for ice cream. We high fived one another. The girls seemed upset that they lost. I was glad that we beat them.

The official basketball season started on a Saturday afternoon. We played the Blue Plains team again. The day of the game, the Blue Plains team seemed confident they could beat us this time. The first half of the game, Blue Plains was up four points; the score was 10 to 14. They had a new girl on their team and she played well.

She was tall and could shoot 3-pointers. Sister Little kept telling us to keep our hands up, which was the only way we could block their players from shooting the ball. Cammi was the guard during the first half of the game. She kept trying to shoot the ball instead of passing it to me.

In the second half, with only three minutes left on the clock, the Blue Plains team was still ahead. I asked Sister Little if she could put me in as guard. When she put me in the game, she called out one of her plays, the "Everton shuffle." I dribbled the ball down the court, handed it to Cammi, who passed it off to Megan, who finally gave it to Lynn. Lynn faked like she was going to pass the ball and shot a 3-pointer.

We were only down one point. The Blue Plains team took the ball out. One of the players dribbled the ball, but I stole it from her. I went down the court for a lay-up. Fouled by one of the girls on the other team, I shot two free throws. The gym was quiet. I could feel the tension in the air. The score was 15 to 14, with a minute left in the game. We were winning by one point.

The Blue Plains team ran down the court, and Megan stole the ball from one of their players. She ran down the court and scored two points with a layup. The Blue Plains player tried to bring the ball back down the court to score, but I stole it and scored again. The buzzer went off.

The crowd cheered and the game was over. We beat the Blue Plains team again. My team ran around the court giving each other high fives. Winning the game meant a lot to me and my teammates, considering it was our first season and we had never played basketball before. We became close friends by the end of our season.

By the time basketball season ended, we had won eight games and only lost two. I couldn't wait for the next basketball season. I wanted to sign up for the Young Women's basketball team again. It was a great experience and an opportunity to bond with my new friends.

GROWING PAINS

Friday was my favorite day of the week. Every Friday night, I looked forward to roller skating at the Hartford Skating Rink. I loved to roller skate. Most of the teenagers in my complex went to the rink every Friday night. Teenagers from all over Maryland came out to skate. The skating rink was located off of Eisenhower Avenue, only 15 minutes away from my apartment.

Riding in the car on my way to the skating rink, I usually got butterflies in my stomach thinking about the guys at the rink. Sometimes the guys asked me to skate during the couple's skate. Most of them could skate well. I liked holding hands with them and hoped they liked me. When the couple's skate was over, the guy might ask to skate with you again.

On Friday nights, there was always a fight. Hoping not to get in a fight with one of the girls was one of my concerns. Girls wanted to fight if they thought you didn't like them or if you accidentally bumped into them and caused them to fall. The guys fought every week for no reason at all. The Lincoln Heights guys fought the guys from Everton Square.

Both groups tried to outskate each other. They competed with one another while they skated around the rink. The boys from Lincoln Heights wore a black t-shirt with a marijuana leaf on it. The guys from Everton wore a gray t-shirt with a picture of a fist on it. Before the end of the night, both groups got into a big fight. The police were called and everyone had to leave the skating rink and go home.

One Friday night in September 1979, I met a girl named Terri. She was pretty and light skinned with long black wavy hair. She was taller than me and a year older. We skated together all night and became instant friends.

Terri, being an advanced skater, could skate backwards and forward. Her roller skates were expensive, like the ones I saw in the glass showcase.

Every Friday night, she taught me something new: how to skate backwards, do a dance, and spin around. She and I came up with a fancy dance routine on our skates. Sometimes, we'd couple skate together for practice or if a boy didn't ask us to skate. Girls were allowed to couple skate with each other.

After a few skating sessions, I could turn from forward skating to backward skating in no time. Terri and I watched the advanced skaters spin around the rink. I told her to call me "Ebbi," my nickname. Terri and I exchanged phone numbers and talked on the phone every night.

Terri became my new best friend; she was like a big sister to me. Terri and I talked about starting our own skating club. We had a few girls we skated in trios with at the rink. Being on a team meant you could skate pretty well. I asked my mom if she could buy me new skates for Christmas. Terri and I decided to name our skating team "Terri's Angels."

Terri looked into the cost of an embroidered top for the team and called around to several shops for pricing. The top would be stitched with each girl's name. She found out it would cost sixty dollars. That was too expensive. We changed our minds about buying the tops. Instead, all the girls on the team wore the same colored pants and tops each week.

I could always count on Terri to have my back at the skating rink. She wouldn't let anyone mess with me. The girls from the South Side of Everton had a reputation of being tough; they liked to fight. If Terri was there with me, I knew I didn't have to worry about anyone trying to jump me. Most of the girls at the rink were afraid of her.

We talked about the boys we liked at the rink and the girls who hated us. Both of us were virgins and had decided to wait until marriage before we had sex. We made a vow to one another not to "do it" with a boy until we got married.

Terri was my confidant and best friend. She knew all of my secrets when it came to boys. Even when I didn't feel pretty or like I measured up to the other girls, Terri made me feel better about myself. I trusted her and loved her for being someone I could go to.

HIGH SCHOOL SWEETHEART

I enjoyed my freshman year at Everton High School. The school took up the entire block of Maine Avenue. The mascot was the Everton Ram. Our school colors were red and white. The student population was diverse with a mixture of many cultures. Everton High offered so many extracurricular activities: cheerleading, pom-pom team, musical theater, track team, tennis, basketball, drill team, and photography.

Before school started, I auditioned for the drill team and I made it. Everyone loved Everton's drill team. Our uniforms were red and white. We wore a white blazer, white pants, white shoes, a red belt, and red polo. The drill team performed during halftime at the football and basketball games.

Students running and scurrying down the hallways of Everton was the norm. The boys acknowledged one another in the halls saying, "What's up like that?" and "What's up slim?" They also gave each other high fives. The boys at Everton were cute. They passed by me every day without saying hello.

One day, this cute boy walked up to me while I was standing by my locker. I was waiting for one of my friends from the drill team. He was about 5'10" and had on a gray Members First jacket, some jeans, and a white polo. "Hello, my name is Rod," he said. I said, "Hello."

Rod was a senior. I had seen him in the hallways before. All the girls loved him. Rod was handsome with a caramel complexion; he was one of the best dressed guys at Everton High. After we spoke, I smiled and walked to my class. Guys who were seniors didn't talk to freshmen. I wondered why he spoke to me.

The next day, I saw Rod in the hallway after lunch. We smiled and waved at each other. At the end of school day, I had drill team practice so I stopped by my locker to get a change of clothes. Rod stopped by my locker again. "Eboni, you look really nice today."

"Thanks, Rod!" I said, putting my books in my locker.

He stood there like he wanted to ask me a question. Then he said, "Eboni, can I get your phone number? I think you are really pretty." I looked at Rod. I was surprised he had asked for my number and had thought I was pretty. "Uh Sure!" I said. I was flattered that a senior wanted to talk to me.

After drill team practice, I went home and did my homework. I looked forward to his call. Every day after school, Rod worked in Everton Mall at a men's clothing store. He said he would call me when he got home from work around 9:30 pm. I finished my homework, ate dinner, and waited for his call.

Rod called me around 10:00 pm. He apologized for calling me so late and said he had to help his mother with something. We talked on the phone for hours getting to know one another. I fell asleep on him. When I woke up at 2:00 am, Rod had hung up. All I heard was a busy signal.

The next day at school, Rod and I met up at my locker. He asked if he could carry my books for me. It was a big deal for a guy to walk you to class. I blushed while he walked me to my first period class. Some of the girls looked at me like they were jealous he was walking me to class.

Rod and I talked on the phone every night. He made me laugh by imitating characters from television shows, especially JJ from *Good Vibes*. Within a few weeks, Rod and I became more than friends. One night on the phone, he asked me to meet him at my locker the next day at school.

After first period, I saw him standing by my locker. When I got to my locker he said, "Eboni, will you be my girlfriend?" I couldn't believe it. I smiled and said, "Yes!"

As soon as I got home from school, I called Terri to give her the good news. I knew she would be happy for me. Thank goodness she answered on the first ring. "Terri, Rod wants to go with me!" I said. "Ebbi, I'm so happy for you!" she said. She wanted me to have a boyfriend and someone to tell me I was beautiful.

One night on the phone, I told Rod I was still a virgin. He said he wasn't. He said he started having sex when he was 14. If he tried to force me to have sex with him, we would break up. He said I was worth the wait and that he would marry me one day.

After a couple of weeks, I fell in love with Rod. He knew exactly what to say to make me feel good about myself. Every day he told me how beautiful I was and that he loved me. I believed everything he said. He promised he would never cheat on me. It felt good hearing a guy say that I was pretty and that he cared for me.

One day, I finally convinced Rod to go to church with me. Even though he didn't like Mormons, he went with me to make me happy. One Sunday, my mom, Rod, and I rode to church. Rod started "joanin" on the missionaries as soon as we walked into the sanctuary. I couldn't help but laugh.

Rod and I sat on the back row. He laughed at the missionaries' pants and socks, calling them "bammas" because of how they were dressed. I reminded him that we were in church. I said, "Brother Rod, it's not nice to talk about God's people." We both cracked up laughing. The sacrament, music, and the format of the service confused him.

Then, he looked around and whispered, "Why are we the only black people in here?" I didn't have an answer for him, so I skipped the subject. After church, Rod asked my mom if she could take him home. We dropped Rod off to his house. He thanked my mom, waved goodbye, and told me to call him later.

My mom said she didn't like Rod because he was older and more experienced. She never said why being older mattered. Maybe she felt a certain way about him and couldn't explain it. I knew it was her motherly instinct. He wasn't the type of guy she wanted me to date. She only wanted the best for me.

Sometimes Rod's mom would let him use her car to take me out on a date. Whenever I asked my mom if I could go, she said no. She always had an excuse for why I couldn't go on a date with Rod. I hated her for that, but I knew she was trying to protect me from getting hurt or getting pregnant.

Our relationship changed the night of June 10th. Terri picked me up from my apartment to go roller skating. Terri had her driver's license; I only had my learners permit. My mom allowed Terri to drive her car. When we got to the entrance of the complex, Terri jumped out of the driver's seat. I took over and drove. I knew how to drive; I just didn't have my license yet.

"Terri, let's stop by Rod's house," I said.

She replied, "Okay, I want to meet him anyway."

I didn't have to call Rod because he was my boyfriend; I knew he would be home. I wanted to surprise him and give him a kiss. Rod's house was off of Edison Road, on the way to the skating rink.

Fifteen minutes later, we pulled up in front of his house. Terri and I walked up to Rod's door. Walking to the door, we heard a girl yelling from a window. "You think that's your boyfriend, bitch!" Startled and shocked by what she said, we weren't sure who she was talking to. It was dark outside, so we couldn't see her.

She started yelling again. Terri and I figured out what window she was yelling from. It was directly across from Rod's house.

"Your boyfriend is f***ing me!" she said.

Terri yelled back, "Bitch, who you talkin' to? You must be scared hiding behind that window."

"Is that girl named Eboni?" she asked.

I didn't respond. We tried to ignore her and started knocking on Rod's door.

"Rod open the door!" I yelled.

Rod came to the door, greeting me with a smile and a kiss on the cheek. He told us to come inside. Rod could hear the girl yelling, but he didn't acknowledge hearing her. I told him I wanted to stop by so that he could meet my best friend, Terri. The girl continued to yell louder and louder.

She called Rod's name. "Rod, you a cheating dog!

I asked him, What's up with that girl? Does she like you or something?"

Rod chuckled and said, "Naw, she's just crazy. Something is wrong with her." He shook his head in disgust. Terri and I sat on the couch in the living room. I introduced Terri to him. "Rod, this is my best friend Terri," I said. "Nice to meet you," he replied.

We sat talking with Rod for a few minutes. It was getting late, so we headed over to the rink. I gave Rod a hug. When we opened his door to leave, she started talking again. "Girl, I'm gonna kick your ass," she said.

Terri said, "Come on outside and do it! I would like to see you try to do it."

I told her we didn't have time for that ghetto girl. That's what I named her: "ghetto girl." Terri drove to the skating rink. I had a feeling something was up with Rod and that girl. Rod was messing around with her behind my back. After my encounter with "ghetto girl," Rod started acting strange. Something was going on.

The next day, my mom was expecting a letter from Calvin, so she asked me to check the mailbox. The only mail was a notice from the Everton County Health Department addressed to me. I wondered why they would send me a notice. I walked back to my apartment.

"Was Calvin's letter in the mailbox?" she asked. I said, "There wasn't anything in the mailbox." I was afraid to tell her about the mail I received. I walked in my bedroom and closed the door.

Afraid of what was inside of the brown envelope, I opened it. The notice said I should go to the clinic to be tested for a sexually transmitted disease. My heart sank. I wondered if it was a prank. I didn't know who would want to prank me about having a sexually transmitted disease. I was still a virgin.

In a panic, I ran to my mother's room and knocked on her door. "Look at this!" I said. I gave her the notice. She looked at me confused. I told her someone was trying to prank me. "Mom I'm not having sex with Rod," I told her. It dawned on me that the girl must have had this notice sent to me. I was humiliated.

My mom still didn't believe that I was still a virgin. She told me to make an appointment with the clinic. I knew she didn't like Rod and thought he had something to do with me receiving the notice from the health department. I called to make an appointment for the next day.

The next morning, my mom drove me to the clinic. I missed school because she wanted to get to the bottom of this situation. After we signed in, a nurse called us back to be seen. She checked me over just like my doctor usually did. Then, another nurse came in to draw my blood.

A female doctor came in to speak to us. "Mom, we're going to give her an exam. Do you mind waiting outside the door for a minute?" My mom got up and waited outside. I'd never had a pap smear before. I was nervous. I told the doctor I was still a virgin and that my mom didn't believe me.

The doctor asked me, "Are you sure you're still a virgin? The notice was sent to you because someone you know has an STD." The doctor decided not to give me a pap smear because she believed me. She told me to get dressed and called my mom back in the room.

The doctor told my mom I was still a virgin and that the notice must have been sent to me by mistake. I was still embarrassed to have had to go to the health clinic to be tested for an STD. It was one of the most humiliating days of my life. If and when I did decide to have sex, the thought of getting a disease scared me.

On my way home from the clinic, I was convinced Rod was sleeping with "ghetto girl." Rod was handsome, charming, and sexually active. Believing that Rod would wait for me until we got married was naïve on my part. I lived in a fantasy world thinking he loved me and could be faithful. Eventually, Rod called and asked me to stop by his house because he had something to tell me.

One Friday night, Terri picked me up to go skating. She said she could take me to Rod's on the way to the rink. I just knew he was going to break up with me. I guess he didn't want to wait anymore. Terri pulled in front of his house and said she would wait in the car. I told her it wouldn't take more than 10 minutes.

I jumped out of the car and walked up to Rod's door. I was surprised I wasn't greeted by the "ghetto girl" yelling out of her window. Rod opened his door, greeting me with a kiss and a hug. He asked me to sit on his couch in the living room. My heart was beating hard and fast. Rod had a look on his face as if something terrible happened, like a family member had passed away.

Looking at me with tears rolling down his face, he couldn't get his words out.

"Rod what's wrong?" I asked. He came closer to me and said he was sorry. "Sorry about what Rod?" I asked.

Suddenly, he handed me a picture of a baby off of the round coffee table. It was an 8 x10 framed picture of a little baby girl. I was confused. I wondered why he was showing me a picture of a baby.

Rod sat on the couch and then he said, "I had a baby with the girl that was yelling at you."

"What?!" I raised my voice.

"Her name is Brina," he said.

"Are you serious, Rod? So, you've been sleeping with that "ghetto girl" and lying to me saying that you weren't?"

I knew he couldn't be faithful to me. Having a baby was proof enough that he was like the other boys I had heard about. Rod was a cheater. I wanted to smack him in his face, but that wouldn't change anything. What did he see in her that he didn't see in me? I was devastated. I got up and left. I didn't say a word, not even goodbye.

I felt the tears coming fast as I walked to Terri's car. Terri was listening to the radio. I got in the car and slammed the door. Rod followed me out to the car. "I love you, Eboni." I didn't want to hear what he had to say. "Terri, let's go!" Before we pulled off, I said, "Goodbye, Rod. Go tell that to your baby's mother!"

The thought of him sleeping with that girl made me mad. Rod can have Brina. Terri asked me, "Are you okay?" I told her, "Rod was sleeping with the girl who was yelling out of the window the other night."

Rod was a no-good dog just like the rest of the guys. My heart was broken. I didn't want to ever fall in love again. I should have listened to my mom. Rod was no good for me. On the way to the rink, Terri tried to make me laugh so that I wouldn't cry.

We had fun at the skating rink. By the end of the night, I was feeling better. Rod had really hurt me. I never knew someone who said they loved me would hurt me so bad.

WRECKLESS NIGHT

By my junior year at Everton High School, I was driving. Rod and I had broken up. I stayed busy to avoid thinking about him and his baby mamma. Sometimes, I drove to Everton Mall after school just to walk around. I avoided seeing him at the store where he worked.

One day, a lady approached me as I was coming out of one of the stores. She asked me if I had ever modeled before, and I told her I had. Her name was Linda, and she was a modeling agent. Linda was pretty. She was tall, skinny, and had long hair. I gave her my telephone number and told her to call me. I was flattered. Even though I didn't think I was pretty or model material.

The next day, Linda called me to give me the audition schedule. Terri said she would take me to the audition on Drexel Avenue in downtown Lincoln. I wore a cute red dress and red heels. We pulled up in front of the tall brown brick building; it looked like an apartment high rise. There was a handwritten sign taped to the front door, so I knew I was in the right place.

I got out of the car and waved goodbye to Terri. She was going to come back and pick me up in an hour. When I entered the building, I followed the signs to the second floor. The audition was in a large conference room. I saw 10 ladies who looked like professional models when I walked into the room. They were at least 5 feet 10 inches tall. Some had long hair, and others had short hair.

The models were standing around the room talking to one another, and soft music was playing in the background. Linda was walking around the room with a pad of paper and pencil in her hand. Then, she turned the music down and asked everyone to sit down at the conference table. She had our attention.

"I would like to see each person audition for an upcoming fashion show. Everyone should have a number," she said. Linda pushed the play button on her boombox to start the music. She played one of my favorite songs, Patricia Ross' "If You Don't Forget Me."

Each model walked down the aisle, posing and turning as they walked past Linda. When it was my turn to walk, I used some of the modeling techniques I learned when I was a teen model for Woodies House of Fashion. I walked down to the other side of the room and did a few turns and pivots with my hands on my hips.

After the audition, we all clapped for one another. Linda said she would call us if we were selected. She thanked everyone for coming out. Terri was parked outside waiting for me. When I got in the car, she asked me, "Did you make it?" I told her, "I don't know yet."

Later in the week, Linda called to tell me I was selected to be in the fashion show. I was so happy. My mom didn't seem excited about it. She said I needed to focus on school.

A month later, the models selected for the show started rehearsals. Linda selected a team of eight models made up of 4 men and 4 women. Linda booked the fashion show at MSVP, a club in the suburbs of Lincoln City. With the show only four weeks away, we rehearsed every Wednesday night.

On the night of the show, I arrived an hour early with my 4-inch pumps and my hair in a ponytail. I was impressed when I walked inside the club, even though I felt guilty being inside of a nightclub. Mormons weren't supposed to hang out or go to nightclubs. I felt weird like I shouldn't be there. Maybe I was convicted by the Holy Ghost.

The club was fancy inside. Streams of fancy white lights hung from the ceilings. The black and white modern and contemporary couch and chairs were spread around the room. I knew my mom wouldn't approve of me modeling at the club if she knew. It was just a fashion show. I didn't think it was a big deal.

Linda kicked off the show by welcoming everyone. The club was packed; it was standing-room only. The DJ played and the crowd started dancing. Linda asked everyone to clear a path for the runway. When it was my turn to walk down the runway, I walked out from behind the curtain.

I was greeted with an applause by the audience, which made me feel beautiful inside. With my hands on my hips, I walked to the other side of the club, did a spin and a pivot at the end of the runway, then walked behind the curtain. The show was a hit. Everyone loved the fashions we modeled.

After the show, everyone changed into their regular clothes. I decided to stay and party with Mona, one of the models. It was still early and a Saturday night. She convinced me to stay a little longer to hang out with her at the club. Mona was really pretty and tall. She was 21 years old.

Most of the men in the club were older. They probably thought I was much older or in my 20s. Some of them looked like they were old enough to be my father. A few offered to buy me a drink, but I declined.

When I got off the dance floor, Mona asked me if I wanted to try some champagne. I asked her, "What is champagne?" She handed me her cup and told me to take a sip. Mmmmmmm. I liked it because it was sweet, so I told her just a little bit. I had never consumed alcohol before.

Then, a guy came over and dragged Mona back on the dance floor. I waited for her at the table. Even though I was having a lot of fun, I knew I needed to get home by midnight because I had a curfew. Mona came back to our table and poured the rest of her champagne into my glass.

Everyone was having a great time, so I lost track of time. I started feeling a little buzzed and lightheaded; it was the first time I drank alcohol. I needed to go home. I tried to convince her that we should leave. "Mona it's getting late." She wasn't ready to go. "Eboni, you can go ahead without me. I've met a man." I laughed.

When I left the nightclub, it was cold outside. I rolled up the windows and turned up the heat in my car. I had a buzz from one and a half cups of champagne. My vision was blurry. I was drunk. I knew it wasn't okay to drink and drive, but I took a chance and drove home.

Driving down the highway, I started nodding off to sleep. When I woke up, the only thing I remembered was seeing the traffic light. I drove into a ditch when I fell asleep behind the wheel. A man stopped by my car. "Are you okay?" he asked.

I sat straight up in the driver's seat looking around to see if I had hit anything or anyone. I said, "Yes. Thank you for stopping to check on me." I quickly looked in my rear-view mirror praying the police hadn't been called. I said a quick prayer thanking God that I hadn't hurt myself or anyone else.

Pressing down on the gas over and over to get out of the ditch, I was frustrated. Once I got out, I rolled the windows down so the cold air would help me stay awake. I pulled in front of my apartment building. I took off my heels, got out of the car, and ran up the steps into the building. Hoping my mom was asleep, I opened the door and tiptoed to my bedroom. I made it home by curfew. I was thankful to be alive and glad I hadn't killed anyone. I promised myself to never drink and drive again.

5
LIFE CHANGES

FINDING MYSELF

I worked at the G + H clothing store for women in Everton Mall my senior year of high school. When I graduated, I wanted to go to college. Going to college was crucial because I would be the first in my family to earn a degree. I couldn't decide on a major because I liked fashion and art.

In the fall of my senior year, I delved into my artistic talents when I took art as an elective. Dr. K was my art teacher. If you didn't participate in her class, she would send you straight to the principal's office. She was passionate about teaching art to her students. Dr. K wanted her students to excel in art.

Dr. K played classical music during class and made everyone listen. "Classical music is better than bee-bop," she'd say. Pretty soon, I started enjoying it and found it very relaxing. It sparked my creativity. By the end of my senior year, I had completed a few paintings to put in my portfolio. Dr. K encouraged me to submit my work to several colleges to receive a scholarship.

I submitted a few pieces of my work and won an honorable mention at The ArtView Institute of Design of Lincoln City. Dr. K encouraged me to major in art when she told me I had a bright future as an artist. She inspired me to attend an art college. I applied to several colleges and was accepted into the prestigious Cortham School of Art. The art school was located in the heart of Lincoln City.

The weekends I didn't work at the store, I hung out at The Class Act club with my girlfriend, Sheila. We dressed up really cute to impress the guys in the club. Sheila used to sneak me in the club because I was only 17 years old. She dated one of the managers at the club, so we had the hook up. We'd walk to the front of the line and get in for free. The guys at the door waved us in every time.

We had a blast dancing all night and flirting with the men. They probably had wives or girlfriends at home but we didn't care. It was hard for me to turn down the not-so-attractive guys who asked me to dance; I didn't want to hurt their feelings. Instead of saying no, I made up an excuse. I told them I had to go to the ladies' room. By the time I came out, I hoped they had asked someone else to dance.

The only downside to being in the club was inhaling cigarette smoke. I hated the smell it left on my clothes. I couldn't understand why people smoked. Being a Mormon, I wasn't supposed to smoke cigarettes. It was against the "Word of Wisdom." I had a lot of friends who smoked and I wanted to know why.

Being curious about smoking, I decided to try it. The first time I took a puff is a day I will never forget. I stopped by the gas station (this was when gas was 70 cents a gallon). When I went to the window to pay the attendant, I saw cigarette packs on the shelf. I asked the attendant for a pack. He asked me what kind I wanted, but I didn't know which brand to choose.

I looked at the green and white package with the word "COOL" in all caps, and it caught my attention. I told the attendant which ones I wanted and paid for my gas. The cigarettes were only 75 cents for the pack. Before leaving the gas station, I realized I didn't have any matches. I went back and asked for matches, then I drove home.

I pulled out a cigarette and a book of matches. I struck one of the stems to light it. By the 4th strike, I got a flame and placed it at the end of the cigarette. Not knowing what to do next, I took a big puff and tried to inhale the smoke. I started coughing and choking. Then, I took another puff, trying to make a circle of smoke with my mouth. I couldn't do it.

The smoke made me cough and choke again. Then, I felt a burning sensation in my throat. After 15 minutes of coughing and choking, I realized smoking cigarettes wasn't for me. I put the cigarette out by running water over it in the bathroom sink. I threw the rest of the pack in the trash. That was the first and last time I ever smoked.

After graduating from Everton High, I attended the Cortham School of Art in Lincoln City. There were only three students who looked like me out of 100 students in the entire school. The first few weeks of school were awkward; it was obvious some of the students had never been around black people before. I tried to strike up a conversation with them, but they didn't seem interested.

During the first few weeks of art school, we painted pictures of vegetables. Then, we drew objects with colored pencils. Each day, Professor Feldman introduced us to a new medium. I enjoyed painting the vegetables using watercolor paints. Every morning, I looked forward to painting and drawing new projects in the studio. It was my favorite part of my day.

One morning, I walked into the studio ready to start the day. Professor Feldman said we would be drawing the human body. He asked if we had our Conte pencils and drawing pads, then he told us the model would be joining our class soon. Everyone gathered their supplies and sat at their stations.

A few minutes later, a tall, slender white woman with long black and gray hair walked into the studio. She was nude. The model looked like she might have been in her late 40s. Everyone in the class looked around at one another and tried not to laugh. Then she stepped up onto the long brown rectangular-shaped table and posed. I heard a few chuckles from my classmates.

She draped a piece of red sheer fabric over her right shoulder. Professor Feldman told us to sketch the contour of her body first before we began. I had never drawn the human body before. It felt weird and uncomfortable staring at her naked body. After a while, it seemed like everyone was comfortable and focused on their drawings.

We drew the nude woman's body, capturing her contour, lines, and wrinkles with our pencils and charcoal. Some of my classmates filled up their drawing pads with sketches of her nude body. Professor Feldman asked us to tape our drawings to the wall in the studio. One by one we looked at each other's work. Then we took a break for lunch.

After lunch we returned from lunch, Professor Feldman said we were going to study another nude model. While gathering my pencils and pads, a nude white man about 5 feet 3 inches tall walked into the studio. He appeared to be in his 40s as well. I freaked out. All of the girls started giggling and turning their heads in shame. We were embarrassed to stare at his private parts. I had never seen a male's anatomy up close like that before.

Sitting on the brown wooden chair, he posed with his legs crossed.

Trying to avoid looking at his private area, I sketched a contour of his body and focused on his upper torso. An hour later, Professor Feldman told everyone to place their completed sketches on the wall. After our critique session, it was the end of the school day. We packed up our pads and pencils to go home.

It was a Friday night, and Mona had asked me if I wanted to go to the MSVP club. It was her favorite spot. I wore one of my favorite outfits, a cute striped baggy turquoise and navy pleated pants with a turquoise top. My hair was styled in a snatch back, a popular hairdo in the '80s. It was kind of short and my curls were flipped in the front. Mona wore a red mini skirt and a white tank top. Her hair was in cornrows.

Every time we went to the club, we flirted with the bouncers at the front door to get in free. When I walked in the club, my favorite song was on, "Take Your Time" by the SOT Band. Walking by the dance floor, Mona and I saw a lot of cute guys standing around. They kept grabbing on us to get on the dance floor. The music was jumping, and the crowd was partying. Everyone was having a great time.

When I walked over to the bar to get a glass of water, I saw a handsome clean-cut guy standing up against the wall. He was tall and had a caramel complexion. I sashayed across the room to get his attention. He didn't notice me, so I walked by him again. The song "Just Like Kandy" came on. I started dancing and snapping my fingers, then he pulled me onto the dance floor.

He asked me, "What's your name?" The music was too loud, so we walked over to the bar.

"My name is Eboni," I said.

"So, Ms. Eboni, would you like a drink?" he asked me.

"No, I don't drink." He looked surprised.

I was immediately attracted to him. He was so handsome. When a slow song came on, he pulled me close on the dance floor. With his hands around my waist and mine around his, we grinded on one another to the beat. He held me real tight when we slow-dragged. After the song ended, we walked off the dance floor holding hands. I felt butterflies in my stomach.

We started talking, and my slow-drag partner told me his name was

Mitch. He was 23 years old and had just returned home from the military. I was mesmerized by his good looks. He asked for my phone number, and he gave me his. When I looked at my watch, the club was about to close. Mitch said he had to leave, but he would give me a call the next day. He shocked me, giving me a peck on my cheek. I couldn't wait to see him again.

Mitch called me the next morning just like he said he would. He worked full-time and went to college in the evenings. Every night when he called, we talked on the phone for hours. I asked him if he had a girlfriend, and he said he didn't. I was surprised. As good looking as he was, it was hard to believe him. Mitch asked if he could stop by to see me on his way home from work. I gave him my address and asked him if he knew when he'd be stopping by.

The next evening, I heard a knock on my door. Hoping it was Mitch, I looked in the mirror to see if my hair and makeup were intact. Quickly walking to my room, I picked up a bottle of perfume and squirted some on my neck and clothes.

Walking to my door I asked, "Who is it?"

"It's Mitch," the voice on the other side of the door said.

Smiling and acting giddy, I opened the door to let him in. Mitch looked so handsome in his security guard uniform. He said he had been thinking about me, so he wanted to stop by. "I have something for you," he said. Smiling, he handed me a single red rose. Blushing, I gave him a hug and invited him in.

We sat on the couch in the living room talking about our plans for the weekend. Mitch said he would take me to the movies. An hour later, Mitch had to go. "Eboni, I need to get home. I just wanted to stop by to see you." I walked him to the door, then we kissed. I was falling for him.

Mitch and I began spending a lot of time together. Every week we either went out to eat or to the movies. I avoided any discussion about sex because I was afraid, he'd want to do it. Mitch was older than me, and I knew he was sexually active. We had been dating for three months. I was surprised he didn't ask me when we were going to have sex.

On the phone one night, he initiated a discussion about us being in a committed relationship. I asked him if having sex was a requirement to be his girlfriend. He didn't respond. I told him I was a virgin. The conversation changed after I told him that I wanted to wait until marriage to have sex. All of a sudden, he wanted to end the call. "Eboni, I need to call you back." I could hear disappointment in the tone of his voice.

Later that night, I called Terri to get her opinion. "Terri we've been dating for three months. He wants to have sex. I'm afraid of losing him." I said. "Eboni, you don't have to have sex if you don't want to. If he loves, he will wait," she said. I reminded her about Rod. He said he would wait until marriage, then he went out and had a baby.

That Friday night, Mitch picked me at 7:00 pm for our movie date. He drove up in his 4-door green Chevy truck. Like a gentleman, he opened the door for me. After the movie, we stopped by Shake's Pizza. We cuddled in the booth. Mitch put a quarter in the jukebox and played his favorite song. We flirted, then kissed each other. It was getting late, so Mitch drove me home.

Mitch parked in a space behind my building. Before I got out of the car, he pulled me in really close. He started kissing me on my neck, trying to give me a hickey. My heart was beating fast and hard. Without actually saying it, he wanted to have sex. Then, he said something that stopped me in my tracks. Mitch told me he loved me. It felt good hearing him say those three words. I wondered if he really meant it.

Most of the guys I knew didn't want to wait until marriage to have sex. Besides, I wanted to be with Mitch as much as he wanted to be with me. One of my greatest fears was getting pregnant, but I wanted to be in love and to feel wanted by a man. It was one of the hardest decisions I ever made in my life. Everything felt right when I was with Mitch.

He opened his door and got in the backseat. Then he asked me to get in the back seat with him. "Eboni, I really want you." I didn't want to lose him, so I got in the back seat. One thing led to another, then it happened. We did it. I couldn't believe it happened in the back seat of his truck. Mitch assured me that we were in a monogamous relationship and that I was his girlfriend. He promised to be faithful and never cheat on me.

It was way past my curfew. I fastened my clothes and fixed my hair in case my mother was up waiting for me. We held hands as he walked me up the steps to my door. I pulled out the key to my door. He kissed me, then we said goodbye. I quietly opened the door, praying my mom wouldn't hear me. I tiptoed to my bedroom, closed my door, and laid across my bed.

Thinking about what just happened, I couldn't go to sleep right away. We hadn't used any protection, and I wasn't on birth control. I should have made him wear a condom. Not only was I worried about becoming pregnant, he might have had an STD. So many thoughts ran through my mind. I took a shower. Then, I knelt down beside my bed and started praying, asking God to forgive me. I hoped I didn't get pregnant.

The next day, I checked the mailbox. Calvin had written me a letter asking when I was going to visit him. I hadn't seen him in a few weeks. He wrote to me and my mom almost every week. Over the weekend, I wrote him a letter telling him about my new boyfriend, Mitch. It was easier to tell Calvin about Mitch than my mom. She never liked anyone I dated.

Early one Saturday morning, I drove two hours to the Compton Correctional facility. The facility was surrounded by six feet of barbed wire and stretched over three blocks in the rural community of Compton. A security guard, dressed in all black was seated in a covered booth in front of the jail. He directed me to park in the visitor section of the lot. Before I walked to the visitor center, I pulled out my driver's license and placed my purse in the trunk of my car.

When I got to the front desk to sign in, I told the officer I was there to see Calvin Davis. One of the officers pulled out his walkie talkie and called my brother's name. Another officer told me to show my driver's license and then instructed me to walk through the metal detector at the end of the hallway.

In the open room that resembled a cafeteria, family members and friends sat patiently for their loved ones to arrive. Calvin walked into the waiting room wearing beige khaki pants and a short-sleeve khaki top. Touching the inmates was forbidden, so I couldn't give him a hug. He had to stay on his side of the table. Before we started conversing, I noticed stitches on his left eyebrow.

"Calvin, what happened?" I asked.

"I got in a fight with a dude who tried to stab me."

He didn't want to explain and moved on to another subject. "What's up, Boney?" he asked. After inquiring about everyone in the family, he asked how I was doing in school. He had received my letter and got straight to the point about my relationship with Mitch.

"Calvin, I think I'm in love," I said.

My brother gave me a crazy look. "Sis, this dude got your nose wide open, huh?"

"Yes," I replied.

"For real Boney, dude wants to get in your pants," he said.

"Sis, he just tryin' to get some. Please don't tell me you done had sex with this dude."

I couldn't lie to my brother, so I didn't say anything.

Calvin continued, "If he breaks your heart, Imma kick his ass when I get out." He wasn't playing.

I assured him Mitch was a good guy. "He promised me he wouldn't hurt me."

After hearing Calvin's thoughts about Mitch, we moved on to another topic. In the middle of our conversation, the guard made an announcement that visiting hours would end in 30 minutes. I hated not being able to talk to my brother for as long as I wanted, but we made the best of the situation. When our time was up, I told Calvin I would be back to visit him soon.

Walking back to my car, I wondered if Calvin was right about Mitch. We hadn't seen each other in over a week. He claimed he was busy at work and didn't have time to visit. He stopped calling me every day. Calvin was right. Mitch only wanted one thing.

I called Mitch the next day. "Mitch, how come we haven't talked or seen each other in over a week?" I waited for him to explain himself. Then, I told him that I had missed my period. "I thought you told me you were on the pill?" Mitch's response didn't make me feel any better. Then, he told me he used the pull-out method on the night we had sex. He insisted that I didn't have to worry. But I couldn't help being worried.

A couple of weeks passed; I missed my cycle. I looked at my calendar to see when I last had my period. I started freaking out. I checked my underwear every day for a sign that it was going to show up. I was never late.

Two more weeks passed, but I still hadn't gotten my period. With no signs of my period coming, chances were high that I was pregnant. I called Terri to ask if she had ever missed her cycle. She told me she never had, but she told me not to worry because panicking could keep my period from coming.

A week later, I called Mitch to tell him I was almost certain I was pregnant. "I'm three weeks late." Mitch got quiet on the end. "Hello? Mitch, did you hear me?" He whispered, "Yes." Then he tried to convince me again that my cycle would eventually come. I could tell he wasn't happy with the news.

By the end of the week, I had planned to take a pregnancy test at the clinic. I asked Terri to take me because I felt sick on my stomach. After we signed in with the receptionist, she directed us to the waiting area. A nurse called my name and took me in the back and drew my blood. She told me to come back in 48 hours. Terri and I left the clinic both anxious about the results.

I felt nauseated every day and couldn't keep anything in my stomach. Three days later, Terri took me back to the clinic to get my results. On the way there, she pulled over a couple of times so that I could throw up. We pulled up to the clinic and signed in with the receptionist. My pregnancy test results were in. When my name was called, the nurse walked us to the back. I sat on the edge of the bed and waited for the results.

She pulled out the results."Eboni Davis, you are pregnant." Terri and I looked at each other. Then, I burst into tears. They both tried to console me. The nurse gave me a tissue and Terri held my hand. They assured me that everything would be okay. After pulling myself together, we left the clinic. Terri took me home.

When I got home, I went straight to bed. Later that afternoon, I woke up to eat a sandwich, praying I wouldn't throw up again. I woke up to a noise I heard coming from the living room. My mom had come home from work. If I told my mom I was pregnant that would ruin her day.

Pretending to be asleep, I heard my mom say, "Ebbi, are you okay?"

"Yes. I'm fine, just tired." I replied.

The next morning, I didn't feel well enough to go to school. I stayed in the bathroom all morning with my head over the sink. My mom heard me vomiting. Knocking on the door, she asked if I was pregnant. I didn't respond and wondered how she knew. I stayed in the bathroom with the door locked shut and my head hanging over the bathroom sink. My mom wanted to know what was going on with me. I told her I was fine, but she knew better.

Leaning over the bathroom sink, I felt so sick. I couldn't even stand up. The thought of raising my child alone made me want to cry. Even though Mitch and I hadn't known each other that long. He'd better not say anything crazy, like the baby wasn't his. If he did, I would smack him. I didn't know how I was going to tell my mom I was pregnant.

I waited until I heard her leave the house before I came out of the bathroom. While the coast was clear, I used the phone in the kitchen to call Mitch. He wasn't at home. I couldn't wait to tell him the results of my pregnancy test.

Later that evening, I called him again. As soon as he picked up, I said, "Mitch, I'm pregnant!" I started crying. He tried to calm me down, reassuring me that he would be there for me. "Eboni, I'm not going anywhere. We will get through this. I'll be there for you and my child," he said.

Surprisingly, Mitch made me feel a little better. He asked me when the baby was due. We talked for hours about our relationship and our new baby. I knew at some point I would have to tell my mother. Before she got home from work, I wrote her a note and placed it on her bed.

Later that evening, I heard the door open. She walked straight to her bedroom. I stayed in bed and pretended to be asleep. The note read:

Dear Mom,

You were right. I'm pregnant. I'm sorry to disappoint you. The baby's father's name is Mitch.

I sat on my bed waiting for her to come to my room. I'm sure she would knock on my door in a few minutes after reading my note. She was probably on the phone telling Mamma G that I was pregnant. I couldn't wait any longer to give her the news. I tiptoed down the hallway to her bedroom. As I approached her door, I could hear she was on the phone so I went back to my room.

Ten minutes later, I heard three knocks on my door. "Eboni," she said. I jumped to answer her and opened my door. "Yes."

Reaching out to me with unconditional love, she hugged me. I could see the disappointment in her face. She didn't know anything about Mitch. Plus, she always wanted me to have kids the traditional way, after getting married.

"I read your note. You're still my baby, and I love you," she said.

I started crying because I didn't want to disappoint her. When she asked me about Mitch, I told her everything she wanted to know. "Mitch is a good guy. He just returned home from the Navy. He is in school and has a full-time job." She listened as I painted a perfect picture of the father of my child. She had never met him, so she wasn't convinced. "We're going to get married one day," I said.

My mom didn't show any emotion on her face after I told her Mitch's short bio. Her reception was better than the one I got from my grandmother when I told her the news. Mamma G fussed at me for a whole week when she found out I was pregnant. Unlike my mom, she made it very obvious that she was not pleased. Even though she was disappointed, I knew Mamma G loved me and would support me and my baby.

The next day, I got dressed for school. I was determined to go to class, even though I had morning sickness. After I drank a half bottle of Pepto Bismol to keep from vomiting, I felt better for a little while. This went on for three weeks. I was too sick to sit or participate in class. Eventually, I dropped out of art school because I had missed too many days and assignments. As soon as I felt better, I planned to find a job.

The daily phone calls from Mitch had ended. He stopped by to see me every other weekend. I wondered why he did. When he came by, he didn't embrace me and seemed uninterested in me at times. He would barely talk to me when he stopped by. He just sat in the living room and watched TV. I felt like he wasn't happy being in a relationship with me. His visits were short and lasted only 30 minutes.

I checked the mailbox and found a letter from Calvin. Apparently, he got the news about my pregnancy. In the letter, he explained his disappointment in me getting pregnant so young. When he mentioned how he felt about Mitch, he was mad at him. He wrote, "Tell dude if he ever hurts you, I'm going back to jail." At the end of his letter, he reminded me that he loved me.

Mitch took me to my doctor's appointment when it was time to find out the gender of our baby. When the doctor did the ultrasound, he told us it was a boy. Proud that he was having a son, Mitch smiled. On the way home, he seemed to be excited about being a father and said, "I promise. I'm going to be a great father to our son."

Our relationship was on and off over the next few weeks. One day, we were together, then the next, we weren't. I wasn't sure if Mitch was sincere about wanting to be with me. He started hanging out with his boys every weekend. Every day, we argued on the phone. Most of our arguments revolved around him not coming by to see me.

One Saturday morning, I got up enough courage to visit Calvin and drove to the minimum correctional facility in Lincoln Heights. I was five months pregnant. After going through security, I waited in the visitor area. A few minutes later, my brother walked in smiling. The first thing he did was look at my belly, then he shook his head. Then, he put his hand on my stomach and greeted his nephew. "Hello Nephew. I'm your Uncle Calvin."

He was disappointed, but excited about being an uncle. I was prepared to listen to a lecture about getting pregnant. Five minutes later, he tried to reprimand me like a father would do to his daughter. It was too late for that. Then he teased me about the weight I had gained. We laughed. I came up with a funny nickname for myself, Big Boney. The guard made an announcement that visiting hours would end in 10 minutes. We said our goodbyes.

When I got home, I called Mitch to see if he wanted to stop by to see me because I was an emotional wreck and felt alone. He gave me his typical response that he would try. Unemployed and a college dropout, I wondered how bad it could be. Terri suggested I apply for medical assistance, aka welfare. Luckily, I found a program for teen moms at the Everest Regional Hospital for Women. The program paid all of my medical expenses, doctor's appointments, and prescriptions during my pregnancy.

In my third trimester, I went to the doctor's every week by myself. Mitch kept promising me he would go with me to my appointments, but he always had an excuse. Usually, an hour before my appointment, he'd cancel because he'd say he had to go to work. I stopped believing he would be there for me.

It was a hot and steamy summer day, almost 90 degrees. My windows were rolled up with the AC turned on. I sat in bumper-to-bumper traffic listening and singing to music on my favorite radio station. Because I was in my third trimester, the doctor advised that someone drive me to my appointments. I had to drive myself to my doctor's appointment in downtown Lincoln City.

Stopped at the red traffic light, I watched people cross the busy streets. It was lunchtime. When I looked to the right, I saw Mitch walking across the street holding hands with a woman. They crossed to the other side of the street. Then, he hugged and kissed her. In shock, I sat at the traffic light with my hands on the steering wheel, trying to hold back the tears. I didn't move when the light turned green. The cars behind me started blowing their horns.

Still in shock, I beeped my horn over and over again to get Mitch's attention. I beeped it again, but he didn't react. Rolling my window down I yelled out, "Mitch! ... Mitch! What are you doing?" He looked like he was surprised to see me. He stood still on the sidewalk speechless. Mitch watched me as I drove off. The girl he was walking with looked confused.

I continued driving to my doctor's appointment. Seeing him being affectionate with another woman hit me like a ton of bricks. I started crying uncontrollably. After parking in the garage, I sat in the car and wiped the tears from my face. Tears started again, as I walked into the doctor's office. Signing in at the desk, the receptionist looked at me concerned. "Are you in labor? Are you okay?"

I nodded my head to let her know I was fine. If I could tell her my truth, my pain was the opposite of what I told her. Being betrayed was the source of my pain. One of the nurses walked by and saw that I was crying. She asked me if I was in labor. I told her I wasn't. The nurse took my hand and walked me to one of the patient rooms.

Handing me a box of tissues she said, "Are you feeling any pain? The doctor will be with you shortly." I stayed in the room releasing my tears until the doctor came in.

When the doctor came in, he asked me where I was hurting. I didn't have the strength to respond. He proceeded to examine me to identify why I was in pain. They didn't know it was in my heart. It was broken and shattered from Mitch's betrayal.

Unable to speak, I nodded my head yes or no, when the doctor asked me a question. The nurse checked the baby's heartbeat. Lying on the bed, thinking about what I had seen, made me cry again. Especially since Mitch said he couldn't take me to my appointment. Instead of going with me, he wanted to be with her, another woman. I'd never imagined being in a relationship could hurt so bad.

Thirty minutes later, I was ready to go home. Driving back home, I couldn't wait to get in my bed. As soon as I got in, I grabbed a roll of toilet paper from the bathroom. I had used up the box of tissue the nurse gave me at the hospital. I was mad, hurt, and disappointed. Mitch was a liar and a cheater, just like Rod.

A few minutes later, I heard the apartment door open when my mom got home from work. I heard her walking down the hallway toward my room. "Ebbi, are you okay?" "Yes. I'm okay." I didn't want her to see me. My eyes were puffy and bloodshot red. I didn't want her to know that I had been crying. When I thought my mom was asleep, I came out of my room and made a sandwich and a glass of Kool-Aid. Then, I hurried back to my bedroom.

I stayed up late waiting for Mitch's call. He owed me an explanation and an apology. The next morning, he called me non-stop. I waited a couple of days before I returned his calls. He left several messages on the answering machine asking for my forgiveness. It was hard staying mad at him for too long because I didn't want him to leave me and the baby. Eventually, I forgave him for the sake of my child.

MY FATHER, MEL

For the first 18 years of my life, I didn't know where my father was, what he looked like, or if he was alive. Now I was expecting a baby. There was no guarantee Mitch was going to be there. We weren't married, and our relationship hadn't been the same like when we first met. It was painful being fatherless and not knowing my true identity; it had me feeling down some days. All I knew was my father's name. I prayed to God that I could have a happy family one day.

One night after dinner, I was sitting at the dining room table when my mom told me some shocking news. She said my father contacted her looking for me. He had called her and asked if he could stop by to see me the following week. My mom knew how much I wanted to meet him. The expression on her face confused me because she didn't seem angry or bitter that he had called. She explained that she had forgiven him a long time ago. I couldn't believe how receptive she was about me meeting him.

So many thoughts ran through my mind about meeting him. I wondered if I should be happy or mad that he wanted to see me after he'd been gone over 18 years. I remember praying when I was 10 years old that he would come back into my life. Then, I had a dream that he came back and hugged me so tight; he wouldn't let me go. Then, he apologized and asked for my forgiveness. After that, we became a happy family. But it was just a dream.

Finally, after 18 years, he'd called. God had answered my prayers. I told my mom that I wanted to meet with him. I couldn't wait to hear my father tell me how much he loved and missed me, promising never to leave me again. That's what I hoped he would say when we met.

The days leading up to meeting him, I wanted to know why he left. Any excuse he gave was unacceptable. I wondered how he would feel about me being pregnant at 19 years old or if he would care. I pulled out a letter tucked in an old journal I had written when I was eleven years old.

The letter read:

To the father I never knew,

It hurts me that you left me. You don't even care, do you? I'm waiting for you to come back. What did I do to make you leave? You never taught me how to ride my bike. You weren't there when I was sick. You missed my award assembly when I received Patrol of the Year. Why didn't you call? My friends said I should hate you. I'm still here waiting for you to come back. I pray God will touch your heart to come back.

Love your daughter,

Eboni.

One Friday night, I heard a knock on the door. I looked through the peephole and asked, "Who is it?" "This is Mel Jones," he responded. I opened the door. There he was standing in front of me at my door. He was tall, with small beady eyes and a dark-skinned complexion. I told him to come in. As he walked in, I noticed he had a plastic bag in his hands. I introduced myself. "I'm Eboni." He shook his head to acknowledge me.

I directed him to sit on the couch. We both sat in the living room staring at one another. I waited for him to strike up the conversation I was waiting for. He hadn't seen me in 18 years. If he had given me a hug when he walked in; would have been appropriate. That's what I expected. He sat on the couch without saying one word. Mel was different in a strange way.

Mitch and I had gotten back on good terms. I had forgiven him for cheating on me, so he was in my bedroom watching TV. Eventually, he came out of my room to meet my father. Out of respect, he went straight to Mel to acknowledge him and shake his hand. My father stood up and introduced himself. "My name is Mel. Who are you?"

Mitch and I looked at one another. He replied, "My name is Mitch Owens." Mitch sat down beside me on the couch. Then there was dead silence. No one said one word. I kept waiting for Mel to tell me why he was sitting in my apartment. I didn't know what to say to him, and I guess he didn't know what to say to me. We sat on the couch looking at each other for 10 minutes waiting for someone to break the ice.

Eventually, he started talking. "You have a Spanish half-sister I want you to meet." I rolled my eyes and I wondered what she had to do with him being in my home. I waited for an apology from him for leaving me, my mom, and Calvin. I didn't care about his 8-year-old daughter. I wanted to know why he abandoned me. Mitch and I looked at each other. It was obvious Mel hadn't planned to apologize or explain himself.

I glared at him. Then he stopped talking. "With no disrespect, Mel, why are you here?" He seemed shocked and surprised by my question. He didn't respond and started questioning Mitch. "Are you going to marry my daughter?" I couldn't believe him. He had the nerve to say something to Mitch about his intentions.

When Mitch didn't respond, Mel repeated his question. "Are you guys getting married?" We didn't respond. Then, he asked, "When is the baby due?" Out of respect, we answered his questions, but I was ready for him to leave. It was a waste of time. I ended the meeting. "Mel, I'm a little tired, and I want to go to bed." He got up from the couch and shook my hand as if I was a stranger, not his daughter.

What an insult! Walking towards the door, he handed me a brown plastic bag. It was an 8x10 frame with a picture of himself at a nightclub. He had on a brown hat cocked to the side, a brown pin striped suit and tie, and black shoes. "I want you to have this," he said. "Thanks," I replied. I still got no love from him. I opened the door so he could leave. I was more than disappointed at the outcome of our meeting.

After thinking about how Mel made me feel that night, I decided to look on the bright side of things. Even though it took him 18 years, I was thankful for the opportunity to meet him. Maybe not having him in my life was a blessing in disguise. Although, I will never forget how he treated me the first time we met. He had no plans of apologizing or explaining what happened or why he left. So many questions were left unanswered.

MY SON, DEAN

One Saturday, my mom said I could use her car to shop for the baby at Everton Mall. I felt so ugly and unattractive in my maternity clothes. I weighed in at 160 pounds at my last doctor's appointment. The baby was due in 4 weeks. My nose was wide, my neck was dark, and my face was plump and ugly. Walking in the mall, I saw one of my modeling buddies. He was walking into a store.

His name was Herb. He was tall, light-skinned, and had curly black hair. We had flirted with one another at the fashion show. At that time, he said he had a girlfriend. Trying to avoid him, I darted into one of the stores hoping he wouldn't see me. I didn't feel like explaining my situation to him or anyone else. A few minutes later, I looked up and saw him walk into the same store.

Quickly, I started walking around the clothing racks and through the aisles of the store to leave and avoid seeing him. Then, I heard, "Eboni, is that you?" I was caught. Slowly, I turned around and said, "Yes. Hi Herb. How are you? What have you been up to?" We hugged each other.

Then, he looked down at my big belly and said, "I see what you've been up to. Congrats! When is the baby due?" I told him the baby was due really soon. For some reason, talking about my situation made me emotional at times. One of the symptoms of pregnancy is a crying spell. I felt the tears falling down my face. Immediately, I grabbed a tissue out of my purse.

Herb grabbed me and put his arms around me. "Are you okay?" I felt better after a few minutes. Then, I thanked him for holding and comforting me. Before we said our goodbyes, we exchanged phone numbers.

Later that night, I called Herb when I got home. We talked on the phone for hours. He gave me an update on his family, work, and love life. I told him about my dilemma with Mitch. He said, "Eboni I always thought you were beautiful. You don't need that dude. I will be there for you and your son. You are beautiful, and you deserve to be with someone who will love you." By the time we finished our conversation that night, he made me feel one hundred percent better about myself.

Herb said he wanted to spend time with me. Every Friday, he took me to the movies or out to eat. Sometimes, we walked to the park and took pictures of one another. Then he offered to take me to my next doctor's appointment. One night when we talked, he said me and the baby could move in with him. A part of me wanted to accept his offer, but I still had feelings for Mitch. I knew Mitch wouldn't want another man raising his son.

The following week, Herb took me to my doctor's appointment. Hanging out with Herb caused me to have feelings for him. I loved how he comforted me. He rubbed my back and even offered to rub my feet. I felt so special when he was around. It was obvious that he cared about me and my son. "Will you name your son after me?" It took me a minute to compose myself. I responded, "I have to consider what Mitch wants to name his son."

Disappointed that I wouldn't agree to name my son after him, he didn't call me the next day. I called him the following day; Herb admitted to being jealous of Mitch. He said he wished I was having his child. "Eboni, I'm falling in love with you. I don't care that you are carrying another man's child." When Herb said he loved me, I became even more confused.

Mitch and I were together, but I didn't trust him. I wondered if I should break up with him to be with Herb. Life was getting more complicated. I didn't have the same feelings and love for Mitch I used to, but he was my son's father. As much as I wanted to be with Herb, I didn't want to take a chance and end my relationship with Mitch. What if things didn't work out?

Herb invited me to his family cookout. I got dressed in my cute denim maternity shorts and white and black striped top. It was a hot and steamy day in the middle of July. I had a difficult time putting on my sandals because my belly was in the way. After I got dressed, I ate breakfast and watched TV until Herb arrived. When I got in his car, he fastened my sandals for me.

After the cook out, Herb dropped me back home later that evening. I enjoyed hanging out with him and meeting his family. Out of nowhere, I felt a sharp pain in my stomach. Words could not describe it. I yelled out. Fifteen minutes later, the pain hit me again. It took me a minute to get up off the couch. I wobbled over to the beige rotary phone on the kitchen wall and called my mom. She was at her part-time job. I was glad she picked up on the first ring.

I said, "Mom, I think I'm about to have the baby!"

"Ebbi, I'm on my way home!" She spoke with excitement in her voice. Describing the amount of sharp pains, I was experiencing over the phone, my mom confirmed I was going into labor. She told me they were contractions. I was glad I had packed my bag the week before like the nurse had suggested.

Immediately, I called Herb and told him, "I'm going into labor. I will call you when I get there." The contractions kept coming. My mom must have been speeding home. It only took her 10 minutes to get home. Flying through the door, I saw her smiling and excited about her grandson's arrival. "Ebbi, are you ready?" she asked.

Before we left, I called Mitch to tell him I was going into labor. For the first time, he sounded excited and said he would meet me there. "Ebbi, I can't wait to see my son." I grabbed my baby bag and wobbled out the door. I couldn't fasten my seat belt, so I rode without it. I held onto the door while my mom sped down the highway doing 75 mph.

My mom pulled up in front of the emergency room entrance to drop me off. I grabbed my bag and got out of the car while she parked. Holding my stomach as I walked into the hospital, another contraction hit me. I stopped to regain myself. Then, I walked over to the front desk to ask for help. The receptionist pointed me to the labor and delivery corridor.

I signed in at the nurse's station and waited for the labor and delivery nurse to call my name. She called me within 15 minutes. I went to the back to be examined by the doctor on call. They checked me to see if I had dilated. The doctor said, "Ms. Davis, it's time. The baby is on the way." I was so scared. Mitch hadn't made it to the hospital yet.

The nurse took me to a room to change into my hospital clothes. By this point, the contractions were coming every 5 minutes. I could barely withstand the pain. When my mom arrived, the nurse took her to another room until it was time for me to deliver. I didn't want to have the baby until Mitch arrived. He still hadn't arrived yet.

I asked one of the nurses if I could have an epidural. Giving me a strange look, she told me she would let me know. It seemed like she didn't care that I was in pain. Thirty minutes later, another white nurse walked into the room to give me an epidural. She had a smirk on her face that made me feel like she was judging me.

The epidural helped the contractions to subside. Lying in the hospital bed, I heard screams from women down the hall. I tried to remain calm. Then, I called Herb to let him know I was at the hospital about to have my baby. He asked me if Mitch was there.

Herb asked if he could come to the hospital to be there with me. "Eboni, I just want to be there with you." I wished Herb had been there. I knew he would kiss me on my forehead and hold my hand to make me feel better. I told him he couldn't come because my son's father would be there soon. Herb asked me, "Will you give your son my middle name?"

To avoid answering him, I said, "The nurse just walked in to get me. Let me call you right back." I didn't want to hurt his feelings. He had me confused and not sure what to do. I believed Herb was sincere, but I wanted my son to grow up with his biological father. My mom left my room because she couldn't stand to see me in pain. She went to the waiting area until the baby was born. I was all alone when the nurse came to take me back to the delivery room.

On the morning of July 15th, my adorable baby boy arrived. He was 21 inches long and weighed 7 pounds and 6 ounces. I named him Dean. After they cleaned him up, cut the umbilical cord, and checked his vitals, they wrapped him in a baby blanket and handed him to me. I kept kissing him on his rosy cheeks. I checked his fingers and toes.

Then, I kissed him on his forehead some more. When he opened his eyes, it was as if I was waking him up from a dream. Looking at him adoringly, I said, "I love you, Dean. You are mommy's handsome little boy." He was my gift from God.

The nurse told me Mitch had arrived and was waiting in my room. They told him to wait there until they finished cleaning me up. I was undecided about Dean's middle name. A part of me wanted to consider giving him Herb's name.

When the nurse rolled me into my room, my mom and Mitch were there waiting for me. Mitch came over and kissed me on my forehead. My mom came over and asked, "Eboni, how are you feeling? Are you okay?" I was disappointed Mitch hadn't brought me flowers or a gift for the baby.

Finally, he asked me, "Eboni, is the baby okay?" He apologized for not getting to the hospital in time. I rolled my eyes at him and didn't respond. My mom kept her distance from Mitch because she was displeased, he wasn't in the delivery room with me. I told them one of the nurse's would bring Dean to my room real soon.

My mom's eyes lit up with excitement. Mitch looked uncomfortable and nervous around her. He could probably tell that my mom was upset with him. The nurse rolled Dean into my room in a baby bassinet. He was wrapped up tight in his baby blanket and ready to eat. The nurse tried to show me how to breastfeed. When she placed his little mouth onto my breast, I flinched. It really hurt.

Mitch and my mom sat watching; they were anxious to hold him after he finished eating. I kept trying to nurse him, but my milk wasn't flowing like it was supposed to. Eventually, one of the nurses gave me two bottles of formula to feed him. Mitch jumped up from the chair and asked me if he could feed him. He took Dean from me and began feeding him formula from a bottle.

He smiled like a proud new father and said, "Hey son, I'm your dad. I can't wait for you to come home." Dean finished drinking his bottle in no time. My mom reached out her hands, asking Mitch if she could hold him. She held him in her arms, kissing him and telling him how much she loved him. "Look at my precious grandson," she said. She rocked and held him as she walked around my room. My mom was the happiest grandmother in the world.

Watching my mom hold Dean, I thought about how I wished Mamma G could have been there for his birth. She couldn't make it to the hospital because she wasn't feeling well. All of a sudden I felt sleepy and asked, "Can either of you keep Dean for me? I want to take a nap." Mitch and my mom both agreed to take over and care for him. I turned over and fell off to sleep.

About an hour later, I woke up from my nap. My mom was sitting in the chair feeding Dean again. Mitch had gone home. When I woke up, my mom told me she was going to leave and asked if I needed anything.

I told her I was okay. After she finished feeding Dean, my mom handed him to me. I laid him on my chest as he fell off to sleep. My mom kissed me on the cheek and said goodbye.

The next morning, the head nurse told me I could be discharged from the hospital; Dean and I could go home. I was relieved and ready to go home. I immediately called Mitch and my mom to see if either of them could pick us up. Later in the afternoon, my mom was at the hospital to get us. I couldn't wait to get home.

Ten months earlier, my life had changed. Riding in the car on my way home from the hospital, I thought about my responsibility as Dean's mom. I didn't know if I was prepared to be a mother at 19 years old, but I knew I wanted to be the best mom to Dean. I wondered if I knew what it took to raise a child.

As a new mom, there were so many responsibilities I needed to consider: daycare, health insurance, food, clothes, and diapers. My greatest fear was that Mitch wouldn't keep his promise to be a good father to Dean. My son having a relationship with his father meant so much to me. I didn't want him to be fatherless. Even if Mitch and I didn't always get along, being good parents to Dean trumped everything else.

A few months went by. I decided to call Mel to give him the good news about the birth of his grandson Dean. "Hello Mel, you have a grandson. His name is Dean," I said. While we were on the phone, he seemed preoccupied and uninterested. Maybe he was busy at work and couldn't talk. I called him back a couple of weeks later.

I remembered the night we met at the apartment that, Mel said he sold cars at the North West Buick in Lincoln City. I really needed a car for me and Dean. Relying on my mom's car for transportation wasn't what I had planned. I didn't want to keep imposing on her. If he was a car salesman, he could help me purchase a car or at least provide a discount. That was the least he could do.

For over a week, I continued to call him to see if I could stop by the car dealership. When he finally answered, he had an excuse for why I couldn't stop by his job. He didn't seem interested in seeing me or his new grandson. In hindsight, I wonder why I thought my father wanted to do anything for me, given his history. He hadn't done anything for me in over 19 years. It didn't make sense for me to expect anything different.

The one thing I did want was a relationship with him. His actions showed me something different.

The last time Mel and I spoke, he didn't have much to say to me. I reflected on the night I met my father. It had been over three months, and he hadn't reached out to see me or his grandson. The hurt and pain of his constant rejection came over me. I picked up the framed picture he gave me and threw it against the wall. Glass shattered all over me and the carpet. The picture, still inside, was exposed. Then I pulled it out of the frame and tore it into pieces. I burst into tears. Mel didn't want to be a part of our lives, so I shouldn't force it. Our existence didn't matter to him.

To me, he was my biological father and that would be the extent of our relationship. Not meeting him, would have felt better than being treated like I didn't matter. I never called him again. He never called me, either.

THE JOY OF MOTHERHOOD

Dean was my gift from God. The day he was born, I fell in love with his cute round face, adorable eyes, and long eyelashes. He loved to eat. After he finished one 8-ounce bottle of formula, he wanted more. I added rice cereal to his bottle when he was two months old. After constant feedings and sleepless nights, I felt exhausted. Most nights, he kept me up until 2:00 in the morning. The demands of a newborn baby were overwhelming.

He loved to stay up and play all night. My mom told me to sleep when he went to sleep. That was impossible because he never went to sleep; he refused to lay down in his crib. Once, I made the mistake of putting him in my bed. Every night I laid him down in the crib, praying he would sleep through the night. I turned the lights off and tiptoed away from the door. Ten minutes later, I peeped in the room to see if he had fallen asleep, but he was wide awake. He laid in the crib playing with his little toes, so I felt guilty and put him in my bed.

One morning, he gave me the scare of my life. I laid him on my bed to change his diaper. Gathering the baby powder and wipes, I noticed he started turning blue in the face. Then, I saw he couldn't breathe. I screamed at the top of my lungs, calling my mom before she walked out the front door. I yelled, "Mommy! Dean is turning blue and he isn't breathing!"

She ran upstairs to the bedroom as fast as she could. Immediately, she lifted both of his arms. We both panicked and called his name. "Dean. Come on, baby, breath." I patted him on his back with my right hand. Finally, he caught his breath and started breathing on his own. I held him so tightly in my arms. We all cried. My mom sat on the bed for a while to make sure he was okay. He started acting like himself, smiling and looking around. It seemed like he was going to be okay. I kept Dean close to me the rest of the day.

I waited until Dean was one years old before I started looking for a job. My relationship with Mitch was rocky. One day on and off the other. He came over to visit us on the weekends. Deep in my heart, I resented him for not marrying me. Back in the day, when a guy got a girl pregnant, it was his responsibility to marry her and take care of her and the child. Times were different. Mitch grew up with both of his parents in the home, so I thought he would want the same for his son.

Every now and then, Herb called to check on me and Dean. He wanted to be in our lives but wasn't sure how he would fit in. One night on the phone, he gave me an ultimatum to choose him or Mitch. I chose Dean's father. I wanted to make things work with Mitch because he was my son's father, and I wanted us to be a family. Herb stopped calling me. I hoped I made the right decision.

Within a year, Mitch and I moved in together. My mom didn't approve of me shacking up with him. She reminded me about what Mamma G had told her when she shacked up with Mel. When she found out about my plan to live with Mitch, my mom said, "Why buy the cow when you can get the milk for free?" She said he wouldn't marry me. He had never mentioned the idea of us getting married.

Everyone told me the chances of Mitch marrying me were slim to none, but I wanted Dean to wake up with his father every day. It was something I never had. I didn't want my son to be fatherless like me. God knew my heart and the reason why I settled for living with my son's father. I wanted Dean to be close to his father and living under the same roof.

After 6 months, I moved out into my own 2-bedroom apartment. The ebbs and flows of our relationship were challenging to say the least. I wasn't equipped or prepared to handle the conflicts we had. We argued about our differences in parenting and things that didn't matter. Eventually, we stopped talking to one another. Mitch didn't want to marry me. I never felt he loved me anyway.

MOURNING MAMMA G

Mamma G moved in with my mom after being diagnosed with Alzheimer's. My mom and I worked out an arrangement for me to take care of Dean and Mamma G at her home. Putting her in a nursing home was a last resort. Taking care of Dean and my grandmother was challenging at times. Every time he woke up, Mamma G was right there wanting to hold him. Because she had fallen a few times before, I didn't want her holding him unless I was in the room.

She wanted to hold him all day. Her eyes lit up with joy every time she saw him. I wanted her to be happy, so I sat on the couch in the living room while she held him. Lovingly holding him in her arms, she sang the "Little Piggy Song," She'd say, "This little piggy had roast beef, this little piggy had none. This little piggy cried wee, wee, wee, all the way home." I walked away for 10 minutes, then found Mamma G in the kitchen trying to fix Dean's bottle.

I panicked. "Mamma G, I will fix his bottle and bring him back to you!" She looked disappointed that I wouldn't let her do it by herself. I told her, "You can hold Dean as soon as I feed him and change his diapers. If you sit on the couch, I will bring him to you." The last time Mamma G tried to fix his bottle; she almost fell. She walked back to the couch and waited patiently for me. He smiled and cooed at her as soon as she started singing another nursery rhyme.

Alzheimer's took a toll on both me and Mamma G. Her health deteriorated each day. It was difficult seeing her suffer with the disease because she was my rock. I loved her so much. To me, she was the best grandmother in the world. She was kind, loving, and always there for me when I needed her. One of the symptoms of the disease was memory loss. Sometimes, she looked at me as if I was a stranger.

She'd say, "Who are you? What is your name?" Frustrated about the loss of her independence, she'd also say, "As soon as I get better, I'm going to get my own place. You won't have to be bothered with me anymore." She felt like she was a burden and imposing on us. Mamma G had always been independent. Because of Alzheimer's, she had to depend on us to take care of her.

On the second Sunday of each month, we took Mamma G to Mt. Lebanon for communion. She made it clear that she didn't want to attend the Mormon church. After church, my mom surprised her with her favorite meal from Pop's Chicken. Pop's was her favorite restaurant. She loved the two-piece white meat chicken combo, with red beans and rice and corn on the cob. After we ate, she usually went upstairs to her room.

She started falling more. Each day, the disease took a toll on her health. The best grandmother in the world and my rock, was slowly losing her battle with this disease. My mom decided to put her in a nursing home. It was one of the hardest decisions she ever made in her life. She couldn't afford a private nurse to take care of Mamma G. Putting her in the nursing home was best for her health and safety.

During my first visit to the nursing home, Mamma G sat in her chair and stared into space. Since moving into the nursing home, she didn't seem like herself. She didn't talk or respond to me. Seeing her in that condition made me cry. Looking at her frail body, I could tell she had lost a few pounds. When I looked at her face, I noticed it right away. I suspected her weight loss was a result of her not eating, refusing to eat, or being neglected by the nursing home staff.

One month after my visit, my world crumbled. On a Friday afternoon, the phone rang. It was Dr. Chen from the nursing home. "Is this Mrs. Davis?" Dr. Chen asked. "No, I'm her daughter," I said. Dr. Chen gave me the dreaded news. "Mrs. Eugenia Lee, expired this morning at 7:05 am."

In shock, I dropped the phone. Crying out to my mom, I told her to pick up the phone. I yelled down the hallway and shouted. "Mamma G died!" My mom picked up and spoke with the doctor. She began to cry in her bedroom. After calling her siblings and friends, she got dressed to go to the nursing home.

I suspected there had been some form of abuse or neglect by the staff the last time I visited Mamma G in the nursing home. They probably left her alone for hours or days and hadn't changed or fed her. No one deserved to be treated like that. The day she received her wings to go to heaven, she was no longer suffering or in pain. Later that evening, my mom returned from the nursing home. Her eyes were puffy from crying. She went straight to bed.

My mom started calling some of Mamma G's church friends at Mt. Lebanon. Over the next couple of days, several members of the church stopped by the apartment to give their condolences. Some dropped off food and offered to help with the funeral arrangements. My mom wrote a letter to the correctional facility to ask if Calvin could come home to attend the funeral. Calvin had been sentenced to 20 years for attempted robbery. Inmates were only allowed to attend funerals of a parent or guardian; however, the warden granted my brother permission to attend Mamma G's funeral.

Most African Americans called funerals a home-going celebration. Lots of family members and friends showed up to pay their respects to Mamma G. There were some people I hadn't seen in years and others I had never met. It was more like a family reunion. All of Mamma G's children were there. My mom was happy that her older brother, John, was there. He went missing 20 years ago.

Thirty minutes before the viewing ended, correctional officers escorted Calvin into the church. They arrived just in time before her casket was closed. Calvin walked in with his feet shackled at his ankles and his wrists in handcuffs. He walked slowly down the aisle of the church as he approached her casket. My mom and I sat in the pew watching him walk to the front of the church. He kept wiping the tears from his eyes.

Standing next to her casket, he leaned over and kissed Mamma G's lifeless body. Then he said his last goodbyes. After he paid his respects, the officers signaled that it was time to go. As they walked him toward the exit of the church, I saw tears falling down his face. I wanted to go to him and hug him, but I knew I couldn't because the officers were there walking right beside him.

After the home-going service, over 200 people gathered in the fellowship hall at Mt. Lebanon for the repass. Members of the nurse's ministry served and fed our family and Mamma G's friends. She had touched the lives of people from all walks of life. As I sat eating and watching everyone that day, I regretted not telling Mamma G how much I loved her. I realized the importance of cherishing my loved ones while they were still alive because tomorrow isn't promised to anyone.

CALVIN COMES HOME

Six months after Mamma G's passing, Calvin was released from prison. He ended up only serving 13 years of his 20-year sentence. His time was reduced because he worked, obtained his GED, took college courses, and stayed out of trouble. On the day he was released, my mom left in the morning to pick him up from jail. She couldn't wait to have her son come home.

I couldn't wait for Dean to meet his Uncle Calvin, and he couldn't wait to meet his nephew. I stayed at home to prepare for the surprise celebration scheduled to begin at 1:00 pm. We invited family and friends from New York, Philadelphia, DC, and Georgia. All of the cousins, aunts, and other family members started arriving as early as 11:30 in the morning. We had a full house because everyone was excited to welcome Calvin home.

Shortly after 1:00pm, I looked out the window and saw my mom pulling up into her parking space. Some of our cousins gathered by the window watching as Calvin got out of the car. He had on new jeans, a white button-down polo, and new tennis shoes my mom bought him. No longer wearing jail clothes, Calvin looked good. I asked everyone to be quiet and to stay in place until he walked in. My mom walked in first, and Calvin was behind her. When he looked up, everyone shouted, "Welcome home, Calvin!" Calvin dropped his bags and cried. Overwhelmed, he stood at the door speechless.

I ran down the stairs to greet him and gave him a hug. "Welcome home, big brother."

He thanked everyone for the surprise, and then said, "Where is my handsome nephew, Eboni? I want to see him." Of course, seeing Dean was the first thing on Calvin's mind. I grabbed his hand and took him to Dean. Calvin picked Dean up and said, "I couldn't wait to get home to see my nephew. Look at his smile. I'm going to name him 'Cheese.'" One by one, people came over to hug Calvin and welcome him home.

In the dining room were trays of fried chicken, ham, meatballs, macaroni and cheese, and salad. I played Calvin's favorite songs. The celebration ended around 10:00 pm that night. He seemed happy and grateful for his welcome home celebration. He played with Dean while my mom and I cleaned up the house.

The next day, Calvin began a new chapter in his life. While he was incarcerated, he successfully completed a welding program. He felt confident he could find a job within a couple of weeks. My mom said he could live at home until he got on his feet. She insisted that he stayed clear of his old friends from the neighborhood. Then, she let him know that if he got in trouble again, he would be on his own.

PROFESSIONAL CHEERLEADER

Even though I was a single mom, I wanted to fulfill one of my dreams of becoming a professional cheerleader with the Lincoln Raiders. It all started when I was nine years old. Every Sunday, my mom and I sat on the couch in the living room cheering for our favorite team, the Lincoln Raiders. I watched the cheerleaders on television dancing and shaking their big burgundy and gold pom-poms in their cute uniforms. They wore short gold skirts, burgundy tops with tassels on the sleeves, and white boots.

I was 22 years old when I decided to pursue my dream of becoming a professional cheerleader. I called the Lincoln Raiders organization to find out how to audition for the team. With no formal dance experience, I wasn't sure I would make it, but I knew how to dance. The only dance experience I had was when I was on the pom-pom team in middle school and when I was a cheerleader in high school.

I thought the audition would be a breeze. By becoming a professional cheerleader, I would definitely get the attention of a good man and maybe a rich one. There were times I doubted whether I was even pretty enough to audition. When that happened, I called Terri, and she encouraged me. She told me that I was beautiful and pushed me to try out. Terri had been such a good friend to me. She made me feel better about my decision to tryout, so I did.

On September 9,1987, I went to my first audition at Lincoln Stadium. The lady at the registration desk took my name and gave me a white label with the number 217 written on it. I wore my turquoise leggings, turquoise top, a matching headband and high-top tennis shoes. When I walked into the room, I looked around at the diversity of beautiful women from just about every culture. I felt a little intimidated. There were hundreds of beautiful women trying out with only 40 spots on the team.

Over 400 ladies dressed in bright-colored leotards, matching headbands, and dance shoes, stood in line. In the audition room, women practiced their leaps, high kicks, and splits. Some looked like they were professional dancers. Doubt set in and I started having second thoughts about auditioning. I thought about leaving before the process began. I didn't think I could make the team.

On the first night, I made the first cut out of 400 women. Only 200 women advanced to the next phase. Elated I made it to the second round, I purchased a new audition outfit the next day. That night, I wore a red leotard, a white top, white leg warmers, and a gold headband to my second audition.

The team's choreographers worked out with us for an hour, making us do laps around the room, jumping jacks, and high kicks. After the strenuous workout, they taught us a new dance routine with lots of high kicks and turns. By the end of the night, there was another round of eliminations. I was disappointed because I didn't make it to the next round. When I got in the car, I promised myself I would try again the next year.

A year later, on September 11, 1988, I auditioned again. That year, my number was 71. There were 300 ladies at Lincoln Stadium auditioning that year. The first night of auditions, I wore my burgundy and gold audition outfit. This year, I wore hair extensions. By the end of the first night of auditions, I was cut. I was disappointed but I remained determined to one day make the team. I walked out of the stadium and looked forward to auditioning again the following year.

The third year of auditions was on September 12, 1989. For some reason, I felt confident I would make the team this year. There were about 250 women auditioning for a spot on the team. This year, my number was 67. I wore my burgundy and gold audition outfit again. After two hours of high kicks, splits and choreography, the panel directed us to a room and divided us into groups of 20.

Before my group was called, I ran to the bathroom to touch up my makeup and quickly practiced the dance routine. Smiling, I walked into the dance room ready to audition. I hit every step, kick, and spin in the routine. The audition lasted all of 10 minutes. Everyone in my group hugged and wished each other good luck.

An hour later, the judges and choreographers asked everyone to meet back in the dance studio. After thanking us for coming out to audition, the judges called the numbers of the women who made the team. I closed my eyes as I listened to them calling one number at a time. Then, it happened. I heard my number, 67. I had made the team. I was the happiest girl in the world.

After the room cleared out, we met the Lincoln Raiders team captains. When the meeting ended, I ran to my car holding my lucky number 67. Driving home from the audition, I couldn't wait to tell my mom the good news. One of the benefits of being a cheerleader was that I received two complimentary tickets to every home game. My mom was a die-hard Lincoln Raider's fan. Securing a spot on the cheerleading team was a win for both of us.

I decided to trick my mom, so I walked in the house with a solemn look on my face and pretended like I hadn't made it. Seeing the look on my face, she said, "I'm sorry, you didn't make it Eboni." I smiled. "Sike, I did!" We both hugged each other and jumped up and down in the kitchen. "We did it! We did it!" we shouted in unison.

When the season started, my mom attended every home game at Lincoln Stadium. My self-esteem was at its highest during my 2-year stint as a professional cheerleader. I felt like a celebrity. Being a professional cheerleader wasn't just about dancing on the sidelines of the football field, it was also an opportunity to give back to the community.

Raiders cheerleaders participated in community-based events in Lincoln City. Not only was it an honor to be a Lincoln Raiders cheerleader for two seasons from 1989 to 1991, I became a role model for young girls. Once a month, we hosted a meet and greet to sign autographs for young girls and fans, which was very gratifying and fulfilling.

REGRET

Meeting my father, Mel, was the biggest mistake I ever made in life. For so many years, I dreamed of meeting him and longed to have him in my life. I wondered why he still rejected me. I will never forget the days leading up to our first meeting, I was so excited. When we met, I hoped he felt the same way about me. After seeing me for the first time in 18 years, I thought he would want to reconcile and build a father-daughter relationship. For whatever reason, I hadn't seen him since we met. I wondered why he reached out to my mom if he was only going to walk out of my life again.

Out of nowhere, my spirits were low. I was down on myself. I began reminiscing about the night of our meeting and the rejection I felt from my father. I asked God why I had even been born. Ironically, Mel's rejection began to empower me to finally let go and live a full and productive life. I wasn't going to let growing up fatherless deter me from living a beautiful life.

Then, I remembered the encouraging and inspiring words from a sermon I once heard: "Everyone is born to live out God's purpose for their life." Since hearing those words, I yearned to find my purpose. I refused to let being a single mom and a fatherless daughter keep me from living a wonderful life. After I ended my pity party, I became determined to pursue everything I wanted in life.

On that special day in 1992, I stopped feeling sorry for myself, I became inspired and filled with an I-can-do-anything attitude. Immediately, I made a list of short and long-term goals. Feeling determined, I registered for college courses, read self-help books, and listened to cassette tapes of my favorite motivational speakers. No more wallowing in my pain, it was time for a change, a paradigm shift. In that moment, I realized if I wanted to change the trajectory of my life, I had to put in the hard work, time, and energy to make all of my dreams come true.

6
PHASES OF MY LIFE

GOD OPENED DOORS

Even though I stopped attending church and practicing the Mormon faith, my faith never wanted. Mamma G taught me how to pray when I was 8 years old. She told me to pray with a sincere heart, because God would answer my prayers. One of her favorite scriptures she cited was, "Ask, and it will be given to you; seek, and you will find; knock, and it will be opened to you." This scripture was forever etched in my heart. I believed that asking God in prayer worked.

Early one Monday morning, I walked around Benton Plaza filling out applications. Finding a job was at the top of my to-do list. When I applied to the Casual Style store, the manager hired me on the spot. They offered me a cashier position. Working at a retail store wasn't my ultimate career goal; it was a temporary fix until I found something better. One of the perks of working at the store was the 50% discount on clothing. It was a great opportunity to build my wardrobe.

Within six months, the manager promoted me to a sales position. It was a $3 pay raise. As a single mother, any extra money I earned, would help. The managers put a lot of pressure on us, setting weekly sales quotas. I had to persuade the customers to buy clothes that didn't fit or that they didn't need or want. Selling clothes became a game. The more clothes I sold, the more money I made.

One year later, I received a letter from the American Telephone company inviting me to apply and test for a customer service representative position. The company was a major telecommunications corporation located in Abbington, Virginia. They offered great benefits with opportunities to advance. My mom worked for the company for over 15 years. Excited about my new career path, I prepared for the test.

Before I left my apartment, I said a quick prayer and claimed my new job. The headquarters was an hour's drive from my apartment. I needed the pay increase to help take care of Dean. The salary would be an 8K pay raise. The morning of the test, I got in my car wearing my navy-blue interview suit, a white blouse, and navy-blue shoes.

When I walked into the testing center, the receptionist asked for my name and identification and told me to have a seat in the waiting area. One of the employees called me to follow her to the conference room to take the test. After completing my test, the employee collected it and asked me to wait for my results. I felt confident that I passed it.

I heard her scan my papers through a machine. Within 10 minutes, she gave me my results. "Eboni Davis, you passed." She congratulated me and handed me a brown envelope with paperwork to bring with me on my first day. The following week, I received an offer letter from the company to accept the Customer Service Representative position. In the letter the manager instructed me to call the personnel manager to make it official. I put in my two weeks' notice at the store.

Within the first few months at my new job, I received several awards. Selling telephones wasn't my favorite part of the job, but it paid the bills. The pay increase helped with daycare and my household bills. Selling telephones and long-distance services to customers when they called the toll-free number was my primary duty. Working in the call center, I received 50 to 100 calls a day from customers all over the US.

The management team assigned weekly sales quotas; which made my new job competitive and fun. They rang a bell each time a customer service rep met their weekly quota. All of the reps in the office became a family. We helped each other meet the company goals. I was competitive and ambitious pushing myself to sell more than the weekly quota. If we met or exceeded the goals, the managers rewarded each rep at the company's quarterly banquet.

The long commute to the office and the constant change in my work schedule became stressful. It was difficult managing my responsibilities as a single parent. I started applying for jobs with a 9 to 5 schedule and something closer to home. My mom suggested I apply for a job in the federal government. However, completing the SF-171 application process was tedious and long. Looking through the local newspaper I found a secretary position in the human resources department at a government agency in downtown Lincoln.

After I completed the federal application, I mailed it to the personnel office. Fortunately, within 6 months, I received a phone call for an interview. I would take any position they offered me to have a regular 9 to 5 job and be closer to home. Dressed in my favorite navy-blue interview suit and heels, I drove downtown to my interview with the federal agency.

During the interview, the office manager gave me a typing test to assess my speed. My typing speed was 58wpm. After the test, I met with 3 panel members who asked me a series of questions. At the end of the interview, they told me I would receive a call if I was selected. I had a hunch that they liked me and that I would get the job.

The next day, the personnel department called me to make me an offer. God opened another door for me and I was thankful. A few of my team members took me out to lunch to celebrate. Working at the American Telegraph company, I learned how to be a team player to reach a common goal. It was my first job in the private industry and I gained much more than an income. I met new friends who became more like my family.

The first day on my new job as a secretary, I went to a meeting with my new boss. Some of my duties as the office secretary included: attending meetings, answering the phone, typing memorandums, and processing documents using the WANG system. The work wasn't hard, and I knew working in the office as a secretary wouldn't be my final career move. The skills and experience I had acquired over the last few years surpassed what I was hired to do.

Carol, my new supervisor was a single mom. She understood some of the trials and challenges single moms faced every day. Within the first 6 months, she commended me for my work ethic and initiative. Carol submitted paperwork to create a position and higher pay grade, which would increase my salary. My position was upgraded to a personnel assistant position with a 5k pay increase.

They offered to pay for college courses if I wanted to go back to school. I declined because it would have been difficult to find someone to take Dean to his after-school activities. Like most single mothers, I had to keep my child active and engaged in healthy activities. I made so many sacrifices to make sure I could provide for my son.

Soon after my promotion, the office was migrating to the MS Windows environment. Carol suggested I sign up for the introductory class. The objective of the class was to teach everyone about the MS Windows and the Disk Operating System (DOS). After completing the class, it sparked my interest to learn more about computers and a possible career in technology.

An entry level computer position in the government required that I have a college degree. I had inquired with one of the managers in the agency. Leaving the federal government to pursue a career in technology seemed like a good idea, but it was also risky. The salary for entry level computer technicians in the private sector was more than the federal government. But working in the federal government was secure.

I started looking through the "Help Wanted" section in Sunday newspapers and saw an ad for an entry level computer instructor position with a training company, Computer Training, LLC. The company provided on the job training. According to the ad, not only did they provide training, they offered bonuses and incentives for their instructors. I was interested in applying.

On Monday afternoon, I called the training company to inquire about the position. One of the training managers answered the phone. I told her I was interested in learning more about the entry level training job. She asked if I had any experience. After she described the position and the benefits, I decided to apply. What really piqued my interest was the opportunity for advancement.

By the end of our conversation, the woman asked me to come in for an interview. A few days before my interview, I reluctantly told my mom I was thinking about leaving the federal government. The look on her face said it all. She tried to discourage me from leaving my job.

The morning of my interview, I felt anxious and nervous more than ever before. I didn't have any experience as a computer trainer. What if I didn't do well after they hired me? Leaving the government for a position in private industry with no experience was a risky proposition.

On the way to the interview, I had second thoughts and almost changed my mind. It was too late to turn around. Walking into the office, I was greeted by the training manager. She asked me to follow her to her office. After closing the door, she asked for a copy of my resume. The manager was impressed by the list of my customer service awards and my experience.

During the interview, she asked me how much I knew about computers, what software applications I used, and if I had a computer at home. Before she officially ended the interview, she inquired about my involvement in the community. She was impressed with the volunteer work I had done with the Boys and Girls Club. The interview was over and she thanked me for coming in and said she would contact me if they were interested.

Within a week the manager called me to offer me the job. Leaving the government was surely a leap of faith. The training company offered me an entry-level computer instructor position; the salary was 8k more than what I made working in the federal government. Along with the salary increase, they offered health insurance and other incentives. It was the perfect opportunity to transition into a career in technology.

The first few weeks in my new position were extremely stressful. I was up late at night studying computer training manuals and software. Computer instructors were responsible for teaching up to 5 software applications a month. After successfully learning the MS Office suite, the manager assigned me to teach introductory MS Windows courses.

I became proficient and an expert in teaching Microsoft Word, PowerPoint and Excel. The students gave me raving training reviews at every site. After the first year, I became one of the best training instructors in the company. One of the training managers asked me if I wanted to begin teaching advanced courses.

The advanced courses included the Novell Administrator curriculum for students interested in computer networking. I was interested in teaching Novell courses to eventually transition to a system administrator position. Teaching the Novell courses would add valuable skills to enhance my resume. Perusing through the "Help Wanted" section of the paper, I saw several entry level help desk positions. So, I applied.

A month after I applied, I received a message on my answering machine to come in for an interview with CompTech Software Systems. My career path to pursue a technology position was working out as planned. Securing a job as a help desk technician would definitely help me advance to a system administrator. The receptionist greeted me when I walked into the office. He shook my hand and gave me an application.

Suddenly, a man walked over to greet me. "Hello Eboni. My name is Don." He escorted me to his office and closed the door. Don drilled me as if I was taking a test. He asked me to explain a few networking terms, topology, software, and hardware. It was exhausting. I was nervous and not sure if I answered correctly. At the end of the interview, Don said he would call me within a week. Three weeks passed and no call from CompTech Software Systems, or Don.

The very next day, I listened to Don's message on my answering machine. He asked me to return his call. Anxious, I called him the next day. Don answered the phone. "Eboni. Are you still interested in the help desk position?" Excited, I responded, "Yes. I am very interested." He offered me the job over the phone and welcomed me to the Comp Tech team. I thanked him for the opportunity. As soon as I hung up the phone, I thanked God for another opportunity to reach my career goals.

Within the first month on the job, one of the supervisors, Tom, asked me to stop by his office after our morning staff meeting. I walked up to his office on the second floor. I wondered if I had done something wrong?

I knocked on Tom's door, "Can I come in?"

He said, "Yes Eboni, come right in." He gestured to hold on, while he finished his phone call. Then he told me to have a seat in a chair. "I'm very pleased with what our customers are saying about the support you give them. We would like you to visit one of our clients in Puerto Rico."

I responded, "Sure. I would love to visit the client's site." He told me he would give me more details in the morning. The next morning, I picked up an envelope with all of the details for the site visit. I'd never traveled to Puerto Rico before. The first thing that came to mind, was who would take care of Dean when I traveled.

I called my mom to see if she wanted to go with me. She was ecstatic. My mom agreed to watch Dean in Puerto Rico. Dean and my mom were so excited about getting on a plane. It was Dean's first time. The captain greeted us as we walked to our seats. He shook Dean's hand and pinned a pair of his wings on his shirt collar. I never saw Dean smile so big. After the plane took off, we picked out a movie to watch on the plane.

The next morning, I picked up a rental car to drive to the client site in San Juan. My mom and Dean went on a tour. The client site was located on a military base. I installed the latest software patches and conducted a MS Windows training session for their staff. After two days at the client's site, I completed the install and helped them with the new interface. I went back home.

When I returned home from Puerto Rico, Tom gave me additional training assignments: Albuquerque, New Mexico, Detroit, Michigan, Pittsburg, Pennsylvania, San Antonio, Texas, and Morgantown, West Virginia. I had planned my next career move to join their network team. Becoming a member of the team would be a major accomplishment.

I asked Tom if I could chat with him after our weekly staff meeting. After the meeting, I went to his office. "Eboni, how can I help you?" he said. I handed him my updated resume. "Tom I would like to join CompTech's network team." Gladly, he looked at my resume. He responded, "I will contact Keith Smith our network team lead."

Weeks went by and no word from Tom or Keith. One morning, I received a call. He asked me to meet him at his office. Later that afternoon, I stopped by Keith's office to meet with him. He walked me around the computer room to see the network team in action.

Next, we walked over to the server room and he inquired about my technical experience. He asked me how long I had been with the company. Then, he asked me when I could start. Shocked that he even considered me, I said, "As soon as I can!" Keith smiled and commented, "I can definitely get you onboard sometime next month."

I reflected on my journey to a career in technology. Just a few years earlier, I had stepped out of my comfort zone and left my job in the government. I realized that I could pursue a career without a college degree, even though I took a few detours along the way. I would have never imagined stepping out on faith would have taken me this far. I'm forever thankful to God who answered my prayers to live out my wildest dreams.

LIVING ON MY OWN

I learned a few life lessons, when I moved out on my own. Being a single mom with one income, it was difficult balancing all of my financial responsibilities. The list of bills I paid included: rent, utilities, groceries, a car note, car insurance, and day care. I failed miserably at maintaining a budget and living within my means.

That's when I learned the importance of paying bills on time and the value of having good credit. Being a single mom, I never had enough money. It was difficult to pay my rent on time. Every month, I had to rush home to remove the embarrassing pink slip taped to my door. But I always managed to pay my rent before the eviction date.

It was a struggle every month. With no savings in my account and no extra income, I made a few bad financial moves. The only method I used to pay my bills successfully was the rob Peter to pay Paul. Falling behind in my bills, caused me a lot of stress.

With all of my bills piling up, I made another financial move, which put me further behind. I put Dean in a Christian school, knowing that I couldn't afford it. Every day, he was dressed so handsome and cute in his uniform. He enjoyed the first few weeks at his new school. I enjoyed hearing him recite Bible scriptures.

Each night, I knelt down beside his bed to pray with him. Without a pause, he started reciting the Lord's Prayer, "Our father who art in heaven, hallowed be thy name." After we prayed, I kissed him on his forehead and said goodnight. I was so proud of Dean.

By the end of the school year, my finances were in shambles. I couldn't afford to keep him in the Christian school. I asked Mitch if he would help me pay Dean's tuition so he could stay enrolled in the school. He said he couldn't. So, I transferred him to a public school at the end of the school year.

After the first few weeks of public school, he was fine. Dean was a smart kid. He had met a few friends from our complex. By the end of the first marking period, he made straight A's and was on the honor roll. He was in the 2nd grade and got acclimated to his new school in no time.

WHEN I WAS A GROUPIE

One morning, on my train ride to work, I met a guy named Mark. He was tall, dark, and handsome. We talked for a few minutes before he got off at his stop. I asked him if we could exchange phone numbers. He handed me his business card and asked me to call him.

Mark was an intern with Technology Group Solutions (TGS), an IT firm down the street from my office. He lived with his best friend, David Johns. His friend was a professional basketball player for the Everton Bulls. Mark called me that evening and asked me if I was single, married or if I had any children. I told him I was a single mom with a young son.

Before we hung up, he invited me and Dean to the next Everton Bulls basketball game. I accepted. The night of the game, we sat courtside. We had a great time watching the players up close. Dean and I had a great time at the game. The following week, Mark gave me a ticket to a Friday night game.

After the game, he asked me to meet him outside of the player's locker room. I walked to the locker room and stood with him while he waited for his friend David Johns. While waiting with him I said, "Thank you for the ticket. Are you guys hanging out tonight?" David came over to speak to us. Mark introduced him to me and said, "Eboni this is my roommate David."

All of the players were leaving the locker room. Then, Mark asked if I could do him a favor. "Do you mind driving Mennot Denk to his friend's restaurant in Lincoln Heights?" I told him I didn't mind. Mark said his car was in the shop and Mennot didn't have a driver license yet. Mennot was from Nigeria. He was 7 feet 6 inches tall. I couldn't wait to meet him in person. I had never met anyone from Africa before.

Then, I panicked. How would Mennot fit in my small 2-door car? There was no way he could sit comfortably in my car. What was I thinking?

When Mennot walked out of the locker room, Mark called him over. "Mennot! My friend Eboni is going to drive us downtown to your friend's restaurant." I tried not to stare at him. In amazement, I hadn't seen anyone with long arms, legs, and fingers like his.

I knew Mark would change his mind once he saw my car. As we got closer, Mennot started shaking his head. "Where am I going to sit?" Mark laughed and pulled the passenger seat all the way to the front. As if Mennot was a contortionist, he managed to climb into the backseat of the car. He looked uncomfortable but I promised him we would be there in 20 minutes."

Driving as fast as I could, we arrived at the restaurant in 15 minutes. I jumped out of my car as soon as I pulled into a parking space and opened my door. Mennot crawled out of the back seat and stretched his long legs. Mark, Mennot, and I walked into the Ethiopian Cuisine restaurant.

Eight of us sat at the brown round dinner table. They treated us like royalty. The beautiful waitresses clad in their African wraps and dresses took our food and drink orders. Looking around at the beautiful African adornment, I was captivated by their Ethiopian culture.

One of the beautiful waitresses came out with what appeared to be white napkins in her hands. She placed one in front of each person. I picked it up to open it. It wasn't a napkin. It was a thin sponge-like texture, injera. Another waitress bought out several round dishes of meat.

She placed the dishes in the middle of the table. I watched Mennot and his friends dip their injera into the bowl of meat. Then I picked up my piece and dipped it into the bowl. Everyone ate out of the same bowl. The meat was delicious and spicy. I asked Mennot,"What kind of meat is this, it's good?" He replied, "Goat."

After dinner, Mennot caught a ride home with one of his friends. I waved goodbye and thanked him for a wonderful time. Mark and I walked to my car. Driving him home, I thanked him for the tickets to the games. I dropped him off and drove home. That was a night, I will never forget.

I MET MY GRANDFATHER, MALCOM

I wish Dean had spent more time with his grandfather on Mitch's side of the family. I thought my father, Mel, would have been interested in being a grandfather to Dean, but I was wrong. Raising my son with positive male role models in his life meant everything to me. My mom told me that my grandfather, Malcom on my father's side, lived with his girlfriend, Janice. I called her to see if she could set up a time to meet my grandfather, who I never met before.

When I called Janice, she was happy that I called. Then, she asked me, "How are you and the baby doing?" I told her we were fine. I asked her if my grandfather was home and if I could stop by to meet him. "Can we stop by? I want my son to meet his great grandfather?" I asked. "Stop by anytime! Your grandfather will be happy to see you. He hasn't seen you since you were a baby. Your mom told me you were a Raiders cheerleader," she said. That's when she shared that my grandfather had season tickets to every home game.

The next day, I called back to ask him to meet me after the game. "Mr. Jones, this is your granddaughter Eboni. I heard you have season tickets to the Raider's games. I'm a cheerleader for the team. Let's meet up this Sunday after the game." He paused a little, trying to process the thought of meeting his granddaughter for the first time in over 24 years. He didn't expect that he would ever see me again.

Before I ended the call, I asked him if he could walk to the cheerleader's locker room after the game. He sounded excited and agreed to meet me. I couldn't resist asking him if he had been in touch with my father Mel. He said he hadn't seen him in a while. Excited to meet him, I couldn't wait until Sunday.

After the game, I patiently waited by the locker room. I figured he was lost, or trying to make his way through the crowd of fans. Thirty minutes later, he never showed up. Janice had warned me that he had a few health challenges and walked with a cane. I couldn't hold it against him that he didn't show up.

The next day, Malcom offered to take me to lunch because he didn't meet after the game. He said he would pick me up around 12 noon. The anticipation of meeting my grandfather was getting the best of me. What did he look like? Was he tall or short? I hoped he was excited to meet me, as much as I was.

A yellow cab pulled up in front of my building. I saw an elderly gentleman sitting in the back seat. He opened his door and struggled to get out of the cab to greet me. "Eboni. I'm Malcom, your grandfather." Trying to keep his balance holding his cane, he gave me a hug. Then he reached for my hand and kissed it. I felt like a queen. He was dressed "sharp as a tack" wearing a black suit, a white dress shirt and a black bow tie. We greeted one another, then got in the cab.

On the way to the restaurant he kept staring at me. The cab pulled in front of Joe's Fish Market. When we walked in the restaurant, the waiter seated us right away and then took our orders. "Get whatever you want!" he said. I pulled out my paper and pen to take notes and asked him a few questions. The first question I asked, "When was the last time you saw my father?"

With a solemn look on his face, he responded that he hadn't seen him in over 5 years. The expression on his face said it all. I could tell it bothered him. Why he and my father had an estranged relationship, was my next question. I didn't want to spoil our first meeting so I moved on to another topic. The next few questions were about his family roots. Where was he born? What were some of his accomplishments?

My grandfather said he played baseball with the Baltimore Knights, a negro baseball team, in the 1930s. Because of his tall stature, the team gave him the nickname "Big Train Jones." He was a back-up catcher for Saxton Paige. The city of Lincoln Heights featured him in local newspapers.

His claim to fame was being inducted into the WWFG Hall of Fame. Hearing all of his accomplishments made me so proud to be his granddaughter. Then, he shared some not-so-great moments of his life when he faced the calamities of discrimination. He recounted how he and his teammates had to go in the back door of restaurants and hotels because they were black.

Two hours later, it was time for me to get back to work. I really enjoyed having lunch with my grandfather. The waiter picked up our dishes and placed the check on the table. With a smile on his face, he handed me a brown letter size envelope. He told me to open it. It was an autographed picture of him and the Baltimore Knights baseball team.

I read the note he transcribed on the top corner: "To my little girl Eboni, love your grandfather Malcom "Big Train Jones." Reading his note, made me tear up a little. I never in life had a grandfather who told me he loved me. I wiped my tears and placed the picture back inside of the envelope. "What should I call you?" I said. "Call me MJ," he said.

The waiter stopped by to pick up the bill. I offered to pay it, but he refused to take any money from me. He picked up the check and smiled. Pulling a wad of 100-dollar bills from his pocket, he said "It's my treat." He picked up his cane. We got up from the table and started walking towards the door to leave the restaurant. Then, we gave each other a big hug. The yellow cab was waiting outside.

On the way back to my office, we made small talk about the Raiders' football team. The taxi pulled in front of my office building. I asked him if he was going to the game on Sunday; so, he could look for me on the field. He wanted to walk me to the door of my office building but I insisted that he stay in the cab. I gave him a hug and said, "I'll call you later, MJ!" I waved goodbye.

LOOKING FOR LOVE

For too many years I had been looking for love in all the wrong places. Especially from all the wrong men. I never felt worthy enough to be loved. My friends told me to love myself first. I yearned to have a meaningful relationship with a man. Loving myself wasn't as easy as it sounded. It's difficult to love yourself when you have low self-esteem.

I never came out a winner playing the dating game. Being vulnerable, I allowed myself to be played by men not realizing they only wanted to "get some." One of the symptoms of being a fatherless daughter is expecting love from a man knowing he didn't have it to give. Feeling unloved most of my adult life, I attracted the same kind of men. I fell prey to their game and always got hurt.

Meeting men was easy. I met guys almost every day and all day. My problem was meeting the right man who was genuine, had character, and wanted a monogamous relationship. The other quality I looked for was a man who would accept my son. Not only was I looking for love but I wanted a father figure for my son. Most of the guys I met already had children. Some of them were baby daddies' and others were fathers who were involved in their child's life.

Over the years, I seemed to attract older men and I was attracted to them. Older men seemed more mature and established. Or could it be that I was looking for a father figure? I dated a few sugar daddies. Dating an older man meant no drama or infidelity, so I thought. I was totally wrong. They showered me with gifts and made me feel special, but those relationships didn't last, like I thought they would.

One morning I met a guy named Dave at Coffee Trends, a store on the first floor of my office building. I was immediately attracted to him. We bumped into one another walking through the door of the coffee shop.

"Ladies first," he said. He seemed like a gentleman. I got in line to order my coffee. He stood right behind me. I felt him standing so close to me, almost breathing down my neck.

When I placed my order, he interrupted the cashier. "Miss, I want to pay for her coffee." I looked back at him, surprised and said, "Are you sure? You don't have to." "I want to," he said. He insisted on paying for my coffee. After he ordered his coffee, he asked me if I had time to sit and chat. "Sure. I have a few minutes," I said.

We sat at a table, then he introduced himself, "My name is Dave." I said, "Nice to meet you Dave. My name is Eboni." He asked me if I was single. I asked him the same questions. Dave said he was single, an engineer, and a veteran of the Air Force. We agreed to exchange phone numbers. He asked me on a dinner date Friday night. I told him I'd let him know and to give me a call.

On Wednesday, I checked my answering machine. Dave left me a message. "Eboni, this is Dave. Are you free on Friday night?" After Dean went to bed, I returned Dave's call. Before I could finish leaving him a message on his machine, he picked up. We talked for over an hour about lives, careers, and families. Talking with him on the phone, I became curious. I enjoyed our conversation and agreed to go to dinner with him.

On Friday night, I waited outside of my apartment building for him to pick me up. He pulled up right on time. Dave drove a red convertible sportscar. I couldn't help but stare at him when he got out of the car to greet me. He looked good in his white polo shirt, khaki pants, and loafers. Then he opened the door for me. I was impressed. He told me we were going to Copper's, one of my favorite restaurants.

When he pulled into a parking space, he told me to wait until he opened the door for me. Then he grabbed something out of the trunk of his car. We started walking to the door of the restaurant. Dave hid the package behind his back.

The hostess greeted us as soon as we walked in. He gave her his name. We were seated in 5 minutes. The hostess walked us to our table. Like a gentleman, he pulled out my chair. I gave him brownie points for opening my door and pulling out my chair. Shortly after we were seated, the waitress came over to take our drink orders.

"Order anything you want on the menu," he said. Then I recalled what a comedian once said, "When guys tell you to order anything you want, be careful what side of the menu you order from. He might feel entitled to make you his dessert." Dave didn't seem like the type. In time, I would find out what kind of man he really was.

After the waitress took our orders, Dave leaned over to pick up the package he had placed under the table. He handed it to me and asked me to open it. It was a box of chocolates and a card. Blushing, I said, "Dave you didn't have to." "Eboni you are so beautiful. I would like to get to know you better. Let's spend some quality time with one another," he said.

I opened the box of chocolate candy and my card. I got up from my seat and gave him a big hug. "Thank you, Dave! I wasn't expecting a gift on our first date," I said. He responded, "Eboni. Just plan on getting more. You deserve it."

Over dinner, we laughed and told funny childhood stories. Three hours later, the restaurant was about to close. After he paid the waiter, he got up and pulled out my chair. He grabbed my hand, as we walked out the restaurant. We had a great first date.

He opened my door, then leaned in for a kiss. I was attracted to him, so I kissed him. We were physically attracted to each other. Then, he put his arms around my waist, and we kissed again. I pulled back and stopped kissing him; so, we could go home. It was getting late. The chemistry we had on our first date seemed unreal.

We held hands in the car on the way back to my apartment. He turned to WHAV "Quiet Zone" on the radio. When he pulled in front of my apartment building, he asked me if he could come in. I told him no because it was too soon. He got out of the car to open my door for me. I saw the look of disappointment on his face. I opened the front door of my building. He was still standing by his car. I waved goodbye and blew him a kiss.

Over the next few weeks, Dave came over to my place when Dean was with his dad. We talked every day, both day and night. After spending so much time together, I thought we were in an exclusive relationship. What we had over the last few weeks felt like we were in a relationship. I trusted him with my heart. He usually fell asleep on my couch, and then woke up and went home in the morning.

One Friday night, we went to the Chesapeake Seafood Diner. We both loved seafood. While we were eating, I asked him, "When are you going to invite me over to your place?" He paused, then changed the subject. I knew something was up by the way he avoided my question. I felt he had something to hide. It had been over 3 months since we started dating. There had to be a reason why he hadn't invited me over to his place.

He made a few jokes to make me laugh. But I had planned to ask him again before the night was over. We ordered the largest seafood platter on the menu. Our table was full of crabs, shrimp, and drinks. We ate until we almost popped. After dinner, we headed back to my place. He still hadn't answered my question.

On the way home, I fell asleep in the car. I woke up when he pulled in front of my building. He looked at me as if he wanted to say something. I had a feeling it wasn't going to be good. That's when he dropped the bomb on me.

"Eboni, I'm living with someone." I was confused.

"What? Oh, you have a roommate, your mom, an auntie or an uncle? Are you trying to tell me you are married, engaged or living with a girlfriend?" I asked him. He confessed that he had a live-in girlfriend.

Upset, I got out of the car and slammed the door. Trying to hold back my tears, I ran into my building. "Eboni! Eboni!", he called me. I kept walking and didn't look back. "I'm sorry Eboni," he said. I should have known he was just like the other guys, and not to be trusted. I wasted 3 months of my life with a man who was in a relationship with someone else.

The next day, Dave kept paging me. I turned my beeper off and didn't respond. Feeling hurt and devastated, I called a couple of my girlfriends to see if they wanted to hang out on "Lady's Night." Going out with my girls made me feel better when I had problems in my relationships with men. We planned to go out to eat, then hang out at the club.

Before meeting up with the girls at Coppers, I stopped by Everton Mall to pick up some stockings. I walked into the Woodworth Clothing store. That's when I heard a male voice talking to me as I was walking through the women's dress department. "Hey beautiful, you got a minute?" he said. He must have followed me into the store. Walking past the clothes rack, he walked over to me and introduced himself. "My name is Ben."

Ben was kind of cute. I told him, "I'm in a hurry to meet my girlfriends." He asked for my phone number. Reluctant, I gave him my pager number.

I headed to the cash register to pay for my stockings. I didn't want to keep the girls waiting. Besides, I was still heartbroken and didn't want to be bothered with another man. I didn't want to get hurt again.

Speeding down the highway, I made it to Coppers in 15 minutes. The girls and I planned to meet up for dinner at 7:00pm. They were sitting in the lobby, decked out in their cute club outfits. We always dressed to impress, when we hung out at the club. Trina and Linda wore miniskirts so short, if they bent over, their "assets" would show. I dressed a little more conservative than they did. My red sweater dress was knee length and I wore red high heels.

As soon as we sat down to have dinner, the girls asked me about Dave. "Dave is a DOG!" I said. I left it at that. Shocked by the news, they seemed disappointed. Trina chimed in, "They are all dogs!" We were regulars at Coppers and ordered our meals so we could get to the club before we had to pay to get in. Ladies got in free if you got there before 10.

The girls and I made it to Club Rizzo's right on time. Before I got out of the car, Ben had paged me several times. I pulled out my Mobile Tech phone in my bag and tried to return his call. He didn't answer. Why was I still entertaining the thought of talking to another guy anyway? I guess I was a glutton for punishment.

Strutting in the club to the music, my girls and I were ready for ladies night. The same old faces were there from the last time we hung out. It was the same old routine. A guy asks you to dance. You dance with him. He offers to buy you a drink. You accept. He thinks he owns you the rest of the night. Sometimes, he's bold enough to proposition you to go home with him. Then you smack him or walk away.

By the end of the night, my feet were hurting from dancing. Girls night was a lot of fun. We had a blast flirting and dancing with the guys in the club. I didn't think about Dave all night. I left the club around 2:00am. When I got home, I went straight to bed with my clothes on. The club scene was getting old and definitely not the best place to meet Mr. Right.

The next morning, I looked at my pager and returned Ben's call. He answered, excited to hear from me. "Eboni! I'm glad you called. What are you doing tonight? I want to take you out," he said. I couldn't turn down a free meal. "Sure! What time and where?" I said. I told him I would meet him at the restaurant. I didn't want to give him my home address.

He asked me to meet him at The SeafoodCafe at 6:00pm. I took a shower, cleaned up my apartment, did my laundry, and prepared for my date with Ben. I wore a pair of black leggings and a cute oversized green top. Then I threw on a little make-up and curled my hair. I didn't expect he'd amount to anything, other than being a good friend.

Around 5:30 pm, he paged me. I called him right back and he said, "Eboni, I'm still at church. Can we meet at 6:30 pm instead?" Mmmmmmmmm. He's a church man. God had answered my prayers. The girls always said I should find a good Christian man. Mamma G once told me that Christian men were faithful and treated their women with respect.

I got in my car to meet Ben at The SeafoodCafe. After pulling into a parking space, I paged him to see if he was inside. A black 190 Series pulled up beside me. It was Ben. I waved at him and he smiled. He got out of his car and ran over to open my car door. "Thank you, Ben! You're such a gentleman," I said.

We started walking towards the restaurant. He opened the restaurant door and said, "Ladies first." The hostess seated us as soon as we walked in. Ben pulled out my chair. The waitress came over to take our food and drink orders. He said he didn't drink alcohol. We ordered virgin strawberry daiquiris.

Before our food arrived, we started talking about life, religion and relationships. I asked Ben if he was single, where he worked, and what he did for a living. He didn't mind being interrogated. Ben said he was single, 30 years old, and he worked for the federal government as a budget analyst.

Ben seemed like a nice guy. I found out we had a lot in common, especially our views on religion. He invited me to go to church with him on Sunday. Walking me to my car, he said "I look forward to hanging out with you again." Then he gave me a church hug. I patted him on his back and got in my car to drive home.

As I was about to pull off, he rolled down his window. "Eboni. Do you mind if I come by your place for a little while? I really enjoyed your company." Unsure why he wanted to come by, I replied "Sure for a little while." Ben was a church man. I trusted him and felt comfortable allowing him to stop by my apartment. I'm sure he would have been respectful and wouldn't try anything.

He followed me to my place. When we walked in, I told him to make himself at home. I asked him if he wanted something to drink. Then, I turned on the TV, so we could watch a movie. We watched a couple of episodes of *Good Vibes*. Out of nowhere, he leaned towards me to give him a kiss. Then, Mr. Church Man tried to touch me on my breast.

With all of my strength, I pushed him away and asked him what he was doing. Then, he tried to unbutton my blouse. Frustrated, I moved his hand. He pulled me towards him and tried to kiss me on my neck. "BEN! PLEASE STOP!" I yelled. It felt like he was going to rape me.

He tried to lie on top of me. Pushing with all of my strength, I yelled again, "BEN GET THE F OFF OF ME!" Then, I slapped him in the face. He jumped up and looked as if he didn't understand why I slapped him. I told him he had to leave.

"Ben, I thought you were a Christian man." He responded, "I am a God-fearing man but I have needs." I turned off the TV and made him leave. He kept apologizing, leaving my apartment. The next day he kept paging me. I didn't return his call. First it was Dave and now Ben. I took a sabbatical from dating.

Six months later, I was at the grocery store shopping when I met Maurice. He was a good-looking black man with beautiful white teeth, and cocoa colored skin. Walking past each other, he made a comment to me. "What are we having for dinner tonight? What's your name?" I blushed and replied, "Eboni." I replied. Immediately, I felt his player vibe. He was a ladies man. I kept walking.

Checking off the items on my grocery list, I stayed focused on my mission. It was taco night. I got in line to purchase my food items. He stood in the same line behind me. "Can I help you with your groceries?" he inquired. I smiled and told him, "Sure!" I was flattered he offered to help.

I waited for him to purchase his items. Then, he grabbed my basket and walked with me to my car. He asked me out on a date. I lied, telling him I was in a relationship. I needed a break from the dating game. "It was a pleasure meeting you but I'm in a relationship," I said. He placed the groceries in my car and said "He's a lucky man." I blushed and got in my car to go home.

A week later, I was walking to the train station. I heard someone calling my name. "Eboni!" I looked back to see who was calling. It was Maurice, the guy I met at the grocery store a couple of months ago. I was flattered that he remembered my name. Looking like he just stepped out of a magazine, he wore a navy-blue pin-striped suit, royal blue shirt and red bow tie.

He sat next to me on the train. Before he got off the train, he asked if I was still in a relationship. I smiled. He told me he wanted to take me out to dinner. Being polite, I accepted his offer. Smiling, he said "Can I call you tonight?" I gave him my phone number. The attendant announced my stop. I jumped up to get off the train and make my connection to the yellow line.

Later that night, Maurice called me. We talked until 1:00am and agreed we'd meet up at the movies on that weekend. Later in the week, he called to confirm our date. "Are we still on for Saturday night?" I was a little apprehensive about going out with him, but I was curious. He seemed like a nice guy but they all appeared to be nice in the beginning.

Before I walked over to the movie theatre to meet Maurice, I looked in my rear-view mirror to check my hair and make-up. He was standing in line to buy our tickets. I noticed how nice he looked, then I greeted him with a hug. The cologne he had on made him look even better.

It was the weekend; the theatre was crowded. Going to the movies was a great idea for a first date. Maurice bought our tickets, then we headed to the concession stand. I offered to pay for popcorn. He bought the drinks. We walked into the theatre. Luckily, we found a good seat. It was the opening weekend of a romantic movie, *Real Love*.

The theatre was filled with couples. It started off slow but it got better. The movie was about a young couple who met in college but separated when they graduated. Over the next year, they would run into one another. They reunited and married when they realized they couldn't live without each other. It was a beautiful love story; it made me cry.

We decided to grab a bite to eat after the movies. Maurice drove us to TGIS. They made the best steak and potatoes. Waiting for our entrees, he asked me a series of questions. He asked what my favorite color was, when was the last time I traveled, and what was the last book I read. I had never been questioned like this before. It felt more like a job interview. I answered all of his questions.

The waitress came out with our food. I picked up my fork to eat, but Maurice stopped me and grabbed my hand to say a prayer over the food.

"Thank you for the food we are about to receive for the nourishment of our body for Christ sake Amen," he said. His grace was short and sweet. I was hungry and ready to dig in.

I ordered the fried chicken and mashed potatoes instead of the steak entree. He ordered fried pork chops. Being careful, trying to eat my chicken leg, Maurice commented, "Girl, just pick up your food and eat it." I laughed and picked up my fried chicken leg. He accused me of trying to be proper. And he was right, I ate proper to impress him.

The waitress asked if we wanted dessert. We declined and asked for the check. He pulled out my chair like a gentleman. We left the restaurant, and he drove me back to my car. After we pulled into the parking lot, he opened my car door. He hugged me real tight and said, "Thank you, Eboni for a wonderful date. Do you feel up to company tonight?" I told him, "No thanks."

I wondered why guys wanted to come over to your house after they took you out to eat? Was this a new dating trend? I learned my lesson when I allowed Ben to stop by. Then he gave me a peck on my cheek. I closed my door and waved goodbye.

On Saturday morning, I cleaned my apartment before taking Dean to football practice. Maurice called me on Sunday evening. I returned his call after I helped Dean with his homework. He asked if he could take me out on another date. I told him the following weekend would work.

Maurice liked to talk. He went on and on about his job. Then we got into a deep discussion about relationships. Eventually, he asked me if I was looking for a long-term relationship. I replied, "I'm tired of the dating game. I want someone who is sincere, faithful and would be a role model and mentor for my son." He told me he was also looking for a long-term relationship.

By Wednesday night, he called me and said, "Eboni, I really need to talk with you face-to-face." The tone of his voice made me concerned. I couldn't wait to hear what he had to tell me. Friday night couldn't come fast enough so I could talk to Maurice. We planned to meet up at TGIS again. I waited in the lobby for Maurice to arrive.

He walked in and greeted me with a hug. There was a 20-minute wait for a table. The suspense was killing me. Finally, the host called his name and we followed him to our table. He pulled out my chair. When he sat down, he had a look on his face as if something tragic happened to him or someone in his family.

The waiter came over to take our food and drink orders. He grabbed my hand and said, "Eboni I'm about to be a father within a few hours." I never would have expected that kind of news. "Are you married?" I asked. He pleaded with me to give him a chance to explain. I folded my arms and then listened.

According to Maurice, he dated a woman for 6 months. He claimed they weren't in a relationship. They were just hanging out. He said they were just friends. She contacted him 3 weeks ago telling him she was pregnant and that he was the father. One day, the girl's ex-boyfriend confronted him when he was leaving her house. She admitted to sleeping with him and the ex-boyfriend.

He stopped seeing her the day he found out she was still sleeping with her ex. "I couldn't believe she cheated on me," he said. Speechless at what he shared with me; I didn't know how to respond. The waiter came out with our food. While we were eating dinner, I still had so many questions that came to mind. Why didn't he use a condom? I thanked him for telling me about his dilemma.

Being a fatherless woman and single mom, I encouraged him to be there for the child's mom. I knew from first-hand experience how hard it was to raise a child. When I asked him if he would reconcile with her, he hesitated. He said he couldn't forgive her for cheating on him.

The waiter handed him the check. We walked out of the restaurant. He grabbed my hand and kept apologizing while he walked me to my car. After he opened my door, he said, "Eboni. Thank you for allowing me to take you out." His story sounded believable, but I wouldn't know if he was telling the truth. I smiled and waved goodbye.

ONLINE DATING

I didn't give up on finding Mr. Right and a stepfather for Dean. Online dating was the latest trend to finding a soulmate. So, I tried it. Some of my girlfriends had already jumped on board and met a few eligible bachelors. They recommended that I sign up for BestMatch.com. My girlfriends promised me I would definitely find a good man. It was better than meeting a guy at the club.

One Friday evening, I created my online profile to begin my search for Mr. Right. I didn't realize there was a cost associated with the dating site. There was a monthly membership fee of $19.99. So, I created my dating profile which was short and to the point. I uploaded my profile photo, and began looking at pictures of eligible men on the site.

In my first search, I scrolled through several profiles of men on the site. I winked at several guys and I was open to dating outside of my race. Winking and flirting with men was fun and just a click of my mouse. I was hooked. The guys flirted back and sent messages to my mailbox. I politely declined to some because they weren't my type.

One day, everything changed. I logged onto the MatchMade site to chat. I received a direct message from one of my matches. His name was Gary. He was 35 years old and had a great job as an architect. He was divorced and had no children. Based on his dating profile, he checked off on most of my requirements: height, weight, hobbies, family man, and religion. It was at least 90% of what I wanted.

Reading his dating profile, he had been on the site for 3 years. Why hadn't he found his soulmate? There were a lot of single, beautiful, and educated black women on the dating site. He sent me a direct message through the dating site and it read

"Eboni, when I saw your beautiful picture, I knew you were the perfect match for me. The more I read your profile, I felt like I already know you. Is it love at first sight? Please forgive me for being so direct. I want you to know I'm no longer interested in meeting anyone else on the site, but you. Let me know if you want to meet up this weekend. I would love to take you out on Saturday night. I have tickets to see one of your favorite artists."

After reading Gary's message, I blushed. Although, I didn't believe one word he wrote. His message made me feel like he was the player type. He was a good-looking man and he had potential to be Mr. Right. Everything he wrote on his profile, made him seem like he was a perfect catch. Plus, I wanted to see a return on my investment.

Curious, I called him. Gary was excited and said he looked forward to meeting me. The first thing I asked him was if he was ever convicted of a crime or if he was a felon. Then, I asked him about his experience on the dating site. Dating men online was risky for women. It was difficult confirming their identity. You never knew if they were who they said they were.

He shared stories about his experience on the site. "It was frustrating when I met one of my matches in person. They looked nothing like their profile picture." Then, he complained that women on the site posted pictures that were 10 years old. He explained that they lied about their age, height and weight. We talked for an hour and convinced me to go out with him.

It was Saturday night. I gave my mom Gary's first and last name in case something happened to me. You never know what could happen. I could come up missing or dead. His name was Gary Little. Then I got dressed for our date. We planned to meet me in the parking lot at the Everton shopping center. I didn't want him to know where I lived.

Gary pulled up in his silver convertible. He jumped out of his car to greet me; I didn't recognize him because he didn't look anything like the profile picture, he posted on BestMatch.com. I was annoyed. He was also shorter than what he posted on the site. When he walked over to greet me, he was barely my height. Not only was he short but he was bald. His online picture must have been taken when he was in high school.

He opened the door for me. As soon as I got in, he handed me a box of candy and a card. I smiled and thanked him for my gift. It was hard to look past his height and bald head. But he seemed so excited to take me out. We pulled off and he took the Southern Parkway exit off the highway.

I tried to figure out where he was taking me to be on the safe side. I asked him, "Where are we going?" He said, "Blues Valley."

Gary read my dating profile and saw that Rachel Frost was my favorite jazz artist. He purchased concert tickets to see her that night. Eventually, we arrived at the venue. The hostess directed us to our seats through the aisles of the small and intimate venue. Our seats were in front of the stage. I was impressed.

I thanked him again for taking me to see her. Smiling, he reached for my hand and kissed it. When he smiled, I saw a couple of gold teeth. That threw me for a loop. I didn't know what else to expect on our date, so, I braced myself for whatever might come next.

Rachel Frost walked onto the small intimate stage with her band behind her. The seats were so close to the stage, I could reach out and touch her. Listening to the lyrics of her songs, made me want to fall in love. As soon as she started singing, Gary reached over to hold my hand. I tried not to look at him. But I liked how he doted on me. He made me feel special. I yearned to be with someone who would treat me like a queen.

The waiter brought our meals to the table. While we were eating, I noticed his table manners. They were the worst I'd ever seen. I didn't mind him picking up his ribs with his hands, but smacking his mouth when he ate was embarrassing. Everyone could hear him. Then he started licking his fingers. It looked like he was hungry. He finished eating his meal in no time.

I couldn't get past his gold teeth. And he was too short. After the concert, he drove me back to the parking lot to pick up my car. On the ride back, we talked about politics and religion. He turned on the radio and started singing; it took a lot to keep from laughing at him. I prayed the ride would be over real soon.

We pulled into the parking lot. I couldn't wait to get home. He pulled up beside my car and opened the door. He gave me a hug and thanked me for going out with him. I thanked him for inviting me to the concert and dinner. He asked if I would call him later. I lied and said that I would.

Gary was a really nice guy but he wasn't my type. It was my first and last date from the dating website. I had planned to end my subscription by the end of the month. Meeting Mr. Right the old-fashioned way would be my preference.

SELF-LOVE

The next day, I called my girlfriend, Michelle, to tell her about my date with Gary. She had warned me about meeting men online and said, "I told you that you never know what the guy would look like until you met him face to face." She was right. They puffed up their dating profiles, writing things about themselves that weren't true.

Michelle suggested that instead of looking for love, I should start loving myself. At first, I was offended by her comment, but it was true. She wasn't a fatherless daughter like me. I was fatherless and had never experienced being loved by a man. Being fatherless was a constant empty feeling inside. It was hard to explain.

She grew up with a father, grandfather, and uncles on both sides of her family. I envied the relationship she had with her dad. He was always there for her. I saw how he treated her, always so loving and kind. Fathers should be active and involved in their daughter's lives. Their relationship will determine the type of men she attracts.

Practicing self-love was difficult, when you've been rejected by the man who gave you life. The abandonment affected me in ways I couldn't explain. A few of my friends who were also fatherless could relate to how I felt. Some people told me to "get over it" and to live my life.

As a single teen mom and now woman, I realized the void I felt may never go away. But it was time to accept my journey and fate as a fatherless woman. There was nothing I could do to change the hand that life had given me; but pray for healing and deliverance from my self-defeating behaviors.

Seeking advice from a therapist, was my first step to healing. Every Saturday morning, I listened to therapist Dr. Cindy Lewis, on WHUT. Her practice was located in Washington, DC. Most of her discussions were about issues surrounding black women. The morning I tuned in; the topic was the life-long effects of being a fatherless daughter. She and her panel of therapists gave advice to fatherless women that called in. I was one of them.

Taking in every word they said, I turned up the volume on my radio. A few of the panel members were also fatherless. Several women called into the show and shared how being fatherless impacted their relationships and marriages. Some called in to discuss how it impacted their sexual behavior. The panelists shared the alarming statistics of African American women who grew up fatherless.

I could identify with the women who called into the radio segment. They shared their pain of feeling abandoned by men. The self-defeating behaviors they revealed was what I had been exhibiting most of my life. I sat on the edge of my bed listening to Dr. Lewis and the panelist's advice. I'd hope by listening it would help me move past the pain and focus on my healing.

At the end of the radio segment, I wrote down her phone number. Seeing a therapist could help me learn how to start loving myself. When I called her number, I didn't expect her to answer. "Hello this is Dr. Lewis," she said. I panicked and couldn't believe she was on the phone. "Hello Dr. Lewis." "My name is Eboni. I would like to schedule an appointment. I'm a big fan. I listen to your radio segment every Saturday,"

"When would you like to come in? What is your name?" she said.

"Eboni Davis."

"I have an opening on this Thursday at 2:00pm," she said.

Then I asked her, "How much is your counseling session?"

"One hundred and seventy-five dollars for 45 minutes."

That was more than I could afford. But it was worth it. She scheduled my appointment for the following Thursday at 2:00pm. After I made my appointment with Dr. Lewis, I called Michelle and told her I took her advice to love myself and that I had scheduled an appointment to see a therapist.

By Thursday afternoon, I took the train to her office. Dr. Lewis' office was next to the train station. I signed in with her receptionist and then sat in the waiting area. Dr. Lewis walked over to greet me and shook my hand. I followed her down the long hallway to her office. Dr Lewis was a pretty and petite African American woman who appeared to be in her sixties.

Her office was decorated with bright yellow and gold couches and chairs. Scented candles were scattered around on her end tables. She asked me to sit on her couch. It was soft and comfy. Leaning against the bright yellow and orange pillows, I felt comfortable and ready to begin my session.

She asked me, "Eboni, how can I help you?" I explained that I heard her segment for "fatherless daughters." on the radio and that I needed her help to move past my pain and learn how to love myself. She told me that she was proud I made an investment in my healing. Then she assured me she would give me the tools I needed.

I began sharing that I met my father for the first time at 18 years old. Talking about that night made me cry. She reached out to comfort me and then handed me a tissue. I told her I hadn't seen him since then. It took a few minutes to regain myself. Then, I explained how I felt unloved and wanted to know how I could learn how to practice self-love.

Taking copious notes, she looked up to acknowledge she was listening. We went past the allotted 45 minutes. She looked at her watch, but kept writing. After she finished taking notes, she tore the piece of paper from her pad and handed it to me. The paper had a list of self-help books I should read.

She wrote out a list of activities I could use when I struggled with low self-esteem. Before I left her office, she gave me a hug. Talking with a therapist made me feel so much better. She walked me to the receptionist to schedule my next appointment. After meeting with Dr. Lewis, I felt it was time to take responsibility for my healing and begin practicing self-love.

30 DAY SEARCH

I made a vow to never call my father, Mel, again. It had been 15 years since I met him. If he had apologized, I would have forgiven him. As much I vowed to never want to see or hear from him again, I often thought about calling him. If I passed him on the street, I wouldn't recognize him.

Looking for Mel would be my last effort to have him in my life. If I couldn't find him after 30 days, I would give up on reconciling with him. A few thoughts came to my mind before I began my search. One, was that he may be deceased. The other was that he didn't want a relationship with me and wanted to be left alone.

Before I began my search, I prayed, asking God to guide me on this journey. I called Janice to see if she or my grandfather had heard from him.

"Hello Janice. This is Eboni, have you seen my father lately?" I asked.

I could hear it in her voice, she felt bad that she didn't have any information about his whereabouts.

She told me, "Your grandfather and I hadn't seen him in years."

I had no information to begin my search. That was a major setback. Why would he not be in touch with his father? If his own father didn't know his whereabouts, that made my search complicated. Janice told me he had a bout with the police a few years back. He had been arrested in Everton County. She wasn't sure if he spent time in jail.

During week 1 of my search, I called the circuit court of Everton to see if I could receive information about his arrest. The clerk had instructed me to send a written request to the courts, to receive a copy of the police report. The report would provide information about his last residence, age, date of birth, and the reason for his arrest.

Looking for the court document, I checked the mailbox every day.

Then, I subscribed to one of the people finder services. It was $20 a month. Using the online search engine, I looked up his name. There were 20 Mel Jones in the list of results. Frustrated, I had run into a dead end and I was ready to give up. It seemed impossible to find him without a social security number or last known address.

By day 14, I received the police report showing his last known residence, his date of birth, height, and weight. It was helpful to know his last known address. I wrote down the address and used another search engine to find him. Unfortunately, there were several Mel Jones listed with the same address. I printed the list of the results.

On day 20 of my search, I contacted the car dealership where he last worked, Northeast Honda of Lincoln City. The manager said the employee records were archived in a trailer on the dealership lot. He advised he couldn't disclose any information about my father without his permission. I ran into another dead end. My search was coming close to the end.

On day 25, I made a call to one of the names on the list from the online search engine. There were 5 pages of Mel Jones who lived in MD. I didn't have anything to lose calling a few of the names on the list. The thought of making random calls, made me nervous. But I had to be diligent in my search.

Before making the first call, I wrote out a script of what I would say when someone answered the phone. I picked up the phone and called the first name on the list. My heart was racing as I waited for someone to answer the phone on the other end. After the 4th ring, someone finally answered.

"Hello." A man answered.

"Hello, my name is Eboni. May I speak with Mel Jones?

I'm looking for my father Mel Malcom Jones," I said. There was dead silence and then he responded.

"My name is Mel Joseph Jones. Sorry, you have the wrong Mel Jones."

I apologized for calling and hung up the telephone. Disappointed it wasn't my father, I didn't want to call another number on the list.

On day 29, I thought about hiring a detective. I looked through the yellow pages to find one. Then I called one of the private investigators in the book and determined that the fees were higher than what I wanted to pay. Their hourly rate was $75 an hour. It wasn't worth it.

By day 30, I gave up on my search to find Mel. I gathered all of my documents and put them in a brown envelope and placed it under my bed. After ending my search, I closed that chapter of my life. Mel gave me life and that was the extent of our relationship. It was time to move on and live out my purpose.

DEAN MADE ME PROUD

Dean always dreamed of playing professional football when he finished college. He started playing when he was 6 years old. His position was a quarterback, and he was good. In his freshman year of high school, he played football for the Everton County Skins, a team for young boys ages 14 and under. Last season, he led the ECS team to the playoffs and won. After winning the championship, the team was featured in the community newspaper.

In the summer of 1996, he attended the Art Freeman QuarterBack Football camp at Westover University in Westminster, Maryland. I borrowed $500 from a good friend so he could attend the camp. The ride to the university was a 2-hour drive from Lincoln City. Dean was excited about meeting new friends and playing football at the camp.

When we arrived at the university, there were 200 kids running around on the football field. There were only 6 African American boys who had attended the camp. Dean carried his football gear, jersey, gloves and cleats to the field and met the staff and counselors of the camp. The counselors had gathered the young men in a circle to introduce themselves.

Soon after the youth and coach introductions, the parents dispersed and left the college campus. My mom and I wanted to kiss him goodbye, but we didn't want to embarrass him in front of the young men. So, we asked him to walk with us to the steps of the dorm and we quickly pecked his cheek.

The week went by fast and it was time to pick Dean up from camp. At the end of the football camp, parents were invited to an awards ceremony. My mom and I drove up early on Friday morning. When we arrived, he was running around on the football field with his new friends. We waved at him and sat in the bleachers until the ceremony began.

Excited, the boys ran around, throwing footballs and tackling one another. "Guys, settle down," the coaches said. By noon, all of the players, parents, and coaches gathered on the football field for the ceremony. Each coach presented their awards based on the football position.

Coach Carl worked with the quarterbacks. He called up his group of 10 boys to come to the front and receive their trophies. Dean walked up front with his group. The coach called out each player by name. One by one, he shared each player's strengths and weaknesses. He told how well they performed at camp.

Coach Carl called Dean's name last. The coach shared how talented he was and that he would have a promising career as a professional football player. Then the coach said, "I would like to award Dean Davis as the Most Valuable Quarterback, or MVQ, of the Art Freeman Football Camp. I screamed. My mom shouted, "Dean you did it!" He walked over to Coach Carl and received a medal and a large trophy.

Smiling from ear to ear, Dean was excited that he won the award. After he received his trophy, he ran over and gave us a hug. We gave him a high five and told him how proud we were. The awards ceremony was over. I thanked Coach Carl for working with him. I never would have imagined that Dean would have received the "most valuable quarterback" award.

Dean said goodbye to his new friends and gathered all of his football gear. We got in the car to head back home. I treated him to his favorite meal at a fast food restaurant. We couldn't wait to get home and share the good news with his dad.

7
IT WAS FATE

CHRISTIAN MAN

Saturday night, I laid on my couch, watched a couple of movies, and ate a bowl of cookies and cream ice cream. To begin my new journey of practicing self-love, I started reading self-help books and spent time alone. The time alone was an opportunity to reflect on the relationship I had with myself, instead of focusing on a relationship with a man. I hadn't been out on a date in a while.

Sunday morning, I got dressed for church because I wanted to recommit my life to God. I was grateful for everything he had done in my life. I visited Evangel Holiness Church, a small local church in my neighborhood. I noticed that the pastor knew his members by their first names.

Pastor Reeves always preached a good message; I looked forward to hearing him every week. The members treated one another like family. After vising the church for 2 months, Dean joined the teen ministry and I joined the adult ministry. The members welcomed us with opened arms. We became a part of the church family.

On the 4th Sunday, the church hosted a celebration, Family & Friends Day. The purpose of the celebration was to invite families from the community to visit the church. It was a perfect day for the event. The sky was clear and it was 70 degrees with no humidity. At the end of the service, members, family and friends would enjoy an afternoon of food and fun in the parking lot of the church.

Every Sunday, I looked forward to attending Minister Harris' Sunday School class. He was my favorite teacher. He taught from the book of Proverbs. When he read the Bible, he dissected each scripture. In previous years when I read the Bible, I found it difficult to comprehend. The way

Minister Harris explained each scripture, inspired me to read the Bible every day.

After Sunday School, I walked into the sanctuary, to find my regular seat on the last row. I looked at the other end of the row and noticed a guy and a young girl. They were probably visitors. At a glance, I thought he was kind of handsome. The young girl may have been his daughter. I tried to stay focused and looked straight ahead at the pulpit.

The praise team opened up the service and everyone in the sanctuary stood on their feet. Every Sunday, the congregation sang along with the choir; praising and worshiping God. Pastor Reeves spoke to the single men and women of the church. In one of his sermons he said, "In Proverbs 18:22, the Bible says. He who finds a wife finds a good thing and obtains favor from the Lord."

At the end of the service, he asked everyone to join hands for prayer. The guy at the other end of the row and his daughter walked towards me, to join hands. We smiled at one another as we held hands. The pastor prayed a long prayer almost 10 minutes long.

During the prayer, I looked up. The guy was staring at me. He quickly closed his eyes as if he wasn't staring. After 5 minutes, we both came up for air. Afterwards, the praise team closed out the service. Everyone was excited to participate in the Family & Friends Day celebration. I was walking out of the sanctuary when the guy walked over to me and said, "Hello. My name is Philip and this is my daughter Monet."

Surprised he came over to speak to me, "It's nice to meet you and your daughter. Are you a visitor?" He said he was new to the area and was looking for a church home. I invited him and his daughter to attend the Family & Friends celebration. Philip told me that he couldn't stay but he would come back the following Sunday.

Over 100 church members congregated in the parking lot excited to begin the festivities. There were all sorts of activities for the entire family: a moon bounce for the kids, arts and craft stations, a stage for live performers, and a DJ. Everyone stood in line for hot dogs, hamburgers, and ribs. Tables filled the church parking lot with side dishes, drinks, and desserts. The youth dance ministry kicked off Family & Friends Day performing a hip-hop liturgical dance.

The next morning, I dropped Dean off to school in the morning and headed to work. I worked at Belvue as a System Administrator for DOD. Everyone on the network team was in the hospital helping end-users because the servers were down. The help desk was overwhelmed with calls. There were server and network issues all morning long.

On my way to help a customer, I noticed someone sitting in a cubicle. All I could see was the top of his head. I walked over to the cubicle and saw it was Philip from church. He said he worked at the hospital as an architect for the Army. What were the chances that I would run into Philip so soon?

I asked him, "Did you enjoy the service yesterday?"

"Yes, I hope to visit again on this Sunday," he responded.

"I look forward to seeing you. I'm on my way to help a customer," I said.

An hour later I walked by the cubicle where he was sitting, he was gone. Another server was down so I headed to the computer room. There were network connectivity issues all day long.

On Sunday, Dean and I went to church. After Sunday School, I walked into the sanctuary. Philip was sitting in the same seat on the back row. I tried not to stare at him but he looked so handsome in his suit. After the praise team finished singing, I heard him shout "hallelujah" and "praise the Lord" from the other end of the row.

The pastor preached a great message. His sermon lifted my spirits. It was food for my soul and helped me make it through the week. At the end of service, Pastor Reeves asked everyone to join hands for prayer. I practically ran over to hold Philip's hand.

The fresh scent of his cologne had me lusting after him. I asked God to forgive me. When we joined hands, it was hard to stay focused on the prayer. Five minutes into the prayer, he squeezed my hand. I squeezed his hand back. When the prayer was over, he kept holding my hand. Then he asked me out to dinner.

Still holding hands, we looked at each other. Pastor Reeves said, "Look at your neighbor and tell them, your prayers have been answered." We looked at each other and repeated what the pastor said, "Your prayers have been answered." We both smiled.

Philip had asked me out to dinner. All I could do is smile and accept his invitation. As I walked back to my seat, he gave me a compliment.

"Don't you look gorgeous?" Trying not to make a fool of myself, I almost tripped over my feet. It was embarrassing.

After I met Philip, I believed Pastor Reeves when he said that God had answered my prayers. First Lady Lisa encouraged women to find a man in the church. Even though the last experience I had with a Christian man was a total disaster. I hoped that Philip was different.

We agreed to meet at the Olive-Green Restaurant for dinner. I was walking in the restaurant, when I saw he had pulled into a parking space. As soon as he walked in, he walked over to greet me. We waited for the hostess to seat us at a table.

It'd been awhile since I had been out on a date. The hostess escorted us to a table. Shortly after we were seated, the waitress came over to take our orders. I waited for Philip to start the conversation. We looked at one another, waiting to see who would say something first and then he said, "Eboni, I love your eyes."

He kept giving me flattering compliments, one right after another. I blushed. It was refreshing to hear someone complimenting me the way he did. I inquired about his relationship status. Philip said he was single and looking for a long-term relationship. He was a single parent raising his 10-year-old daughter, Monet.

We laughed, sharing childhood stories about our first kiss and first crush. Before we knew it, the restaurant was about to close and it was time to go home. He walked me to my car and asked if he could take me out to dinner again. Flattered that he wanted to take me out again I said, "Yes!"

After my dinner date with Philip, I called my girlfriend Michelle. "I had a great time on my date. I think he might be the one. There was something special about him." I wondered, if he could be the soulmate I had been waiting for? We were both single parents and we had a lot in common.

Since our first date, we spent most of our weekends together. He and his daughter Monet stayed over Friday night thru Sunday evening. Philip was a positive role model for my son, a great man and father, that meant a lot to me. He even offered to help Dean with his homework and took him to football practice every week.

Things were getting serious. We attended church together like a family, and sat on the back row of the church where we first met. It seemed like every Sunday Pastor Reeve's sermon was about why single people should wait until marriage before intimacy. Fornicating was a sin and I felt convicted every time he mentioned it.

Every Sunday after church, we went home, watched movies, and ate dinner together. Philip and I stayed up talking late at night. He told me he knew I was his soulmate the first time we met. I felt the same way about him. We hadn't argued or had one disagreement since we'd been dating.

Philip said he wanted to be in a monogamous relationship a month after we started dating. The men I dated in the past avoided the idea of being in a committed relationship. Everything about him seemed too good to be true. I wanted to pinch myself because our relationship didn't seem real.

One Monday morning, I woke up feeling nauseated and could barely get dressed for work. I asked Dean if he could call my mom to drive him to school. Then, I got back in bed. I was too sick to go to work. I hadn't felt this sick in over 15 years.

Concerned that he hadn't heard from me, he called me and said, "Eboni baby, what's wrong? What happened to my morning call?" I told him I felt sick on my stomach. Everything I ate made me want to throw up. He said he'd be right over to take care of me.

He bought me a box of Saltine crackers, ginger ale, and soup. Then, he came into my bedroom and sat on the side of the bed. Rubbing my shoulders and my back, he tried to make me feel better. He kissed me on my forehead. I told him, "Thank you for taking care of me." He turned off the light so I could fall asleep.

Later that afternoon, when I woke up from my nap, I felt better. Philip was in the living room watching TV. Before he left out to pick the kids up from school, I yelled, "Can you stop by the store to pick up a pregnancy test?" I was certain that I was pregnant.

Philip came in my bedroom to check on me. I asked him to put the test on my dresser. I felt like I had to throw up again. Everything I had eaten came back up. He stayed in the room with me to make sure I would be okay.

When I finally crawled out of bed, I grabbed the pregnancy test and went to the bathroom. He asked me if I was sure I was pregnant. Giving him a funny look, I said "We will find out. I wonder how that happened?"

Even though I was worried about being pregnant, I knew he would be a great father. I was sure he would never leave me. He was a good and faithful Christian man.

Philip had been consistent since the moment we started dating. I had never experienced a relationship like this before. Being in a relationship with a man like Philip, was a dream come true. I knew he was faithful to me and he loved me. I was falling in love with him and everything seemed right, this time.

We were becoming a happy family. He taught Dean how to do things fathers taught their sons. His daughter became my daughter. Monet's mother was killed in a car accident when she was 4 years old. We formed a bond. I was her mother and she was my daughter.

The test sat on the bathroom counter. I took the pregnancy test and left it on the counter. It sat there for 15 minutes, so Philip could see the results. He said he'd tell me the pregnancy results. I crawled back in bed and pulled the covers over my head.

That evening for dinner, Philip prepared his famous spaghetti and meat sauce. The aroma made me sick on my stomach. He fixed me a plate of food. I declined because I knew it would come back up.

"Can you check the results of the test? It's in the bathroom on the counter," I said. He went into the bathroom and asked what he should look for. "A blue line!" I replied. I waited for Philip to give me the results. Ten minutes later, he opened the door and walked towards my bed with a smile on his face.

"What are you smiling about?" I asked.

He replied, "I saw the blue line!" He leaned over and kissed me on my forehead.

"Are you sure? You saw the blue line? " I asked.

I was too sick and nauseated to show any emotions. Feeling sick on my stomach again, I leaned over the side of the bed to throw up. The realization of being pregnant hit me, and I burst into tears.

JOY & PAIN

The next morning, I felt better. I was able to stand up without feeling like I had to vomit again. After I took a long hot shower, I felt 100% better. I didn't want to miss another day from work. I got ready for work. Philip was still asleep.

I walked over to his side of the bed and kissed him on his forehead, "Wake up babe," I said. A few minutes later, he woke up. As I walked by his side of the bed, he grabbed me, lifted my top and kissed me on my belly. "Good morning baby."

On my way to work, it suddenly dawned on me that I was going to be a mom all over again. I wasn't married and I was having a baby with someone I had only known for 8 months. Why was I so irresponsible? We'd been together less than one year. Would Philip marry me? There was no guarantee he'd stay.

One night he was preparing dinner, I asked him, "Are you sure you're ready for another child?" He walked over to me. "Yes Eboni. I love you and Dean." Then he rubbed my belly. "Let's get married!" Ecstatic, I couldn't believe he had proposed to me. Lovingly, I said,"Yes!"

Philip was sincere and I believed that he really loved me. He was the kind of man I'd always dreamed of. We held each other tight after he asked me to marry him. The only concern I had was that we hadn't known each other long enough but marrying him would be worth a try.

I scheduled a doctor's appointment with the Lincoln's Family Practice to find out how pregnant I was. My appointment was scheduled for the following Monday. I asked Philip if he would come. He said he'd be at every appointment. Hearing he'd be there for me made me happy.

The morning of my first appointment, we walked into the doctor's office and the receptionist gave me paperwork to fill out. The OB/GYN doctor on call, Dr. Myer, walked into the room and introduced himself. He told us that one of his technicians would give me a sonogram.

Listening to the baby's heartbeat, we smiled and looked at the monitor. He held my hand. The baby was 18 weeks, so I was a little over 4 months pregnant. At the next appointment, the doctor said he could determine the sex of the baby. Philip wanted a boy. I wanted a girl.

On our way home, Philip suggested that we get married right away, before I started showing. He said he wanted to make me an "honest woman." Sounding excited about getting married he said, "Let's plan to get married at the justice of peace. We can have a formal wedding later." I leaned over and kissed him.

Dean and I started spending time at Philip's house in Granville, MD. It was an hour drive from my apartment. Now that I was pregnant, and we were getting married, it made sense for Dean and I to move into his place. His townhouse had 4 bedrooms and a basement.

On September 1, we moved into Philip's home. My girlfriends, Terri and Michelle, helped me pack up my apartment. It took us an entire weekend to move into his home. Dean started fixing up his room, placing posters on the wall. Philip told me to fix up the house anyway I wanted. He told me the basement was where he'd hang out. He called it his mancave.

The first room I decorated was the baby's nursery. Because I didn't know the gender of the baby, I painted the room a neutral color, yellow. It was a color that could work for either a boy or a girl. I purchased decals of baby sheep, to place on the walls. My girlfriend Michelle bought me a yellow baby comforter.

Two weeks after Dean and I moved in with Philip, we got married. I couldn't believe my dreams of finding a husband came true. The morning of our wedding ceremony was the happiest day of my life. It was a beautiful sunny day in October. I did my own hair and makeup. My mother bought me an off-white maternity dress to hide my stomach.

My wedding dress was an off-white long and flowy gown with ruffled sleeves. Philip wore an off-white linen suit. He always looked good in suits and cleaned up so nicely. Dean wore a pair of black dress slacks, a white shirt, and a tie. Monet wore a beautiful pink floral dress with a white lace collar. My mom wore a beautiful rose-colored dress.

On the day of our wedding, the kids and I all piled into Philip's car to drive to the courthouse. My mom met us there. We got married at the Granville County courthouse. When we arrived at the courthouse, we waited for the clerk to call our names. At 1:00pm, she called us to follow her to the small chapel. I couldn't wait to be Mrs. Eboni Steele.

The day we got married was the happiest day of my life. The kids and my mom sat in the pews, when the ceremony began. My mom cried. She was happy for me. After we recited our vows, Philip touched my belly and said, "I promise to always love you and never leave you, Eboni." We were pronounced Mr. & Mrs. Steele.

After the ceremony, we got in our cars and drove to Joe's Seafood to celebrate our nuptials. I ate too much. When we left the restaurant, I wobbled to the car and could barely get in the front seat. Philip had to help me get in the car. Dean and Monet jumped in the backseat. My mom went home.

At my last appointment, the doctor said I had gained forty pounds in 4 weeks. When I looked in the mirror, I didn't recognize myself. My girlfriends told me I was having a girl. They said when you are expecting a girl, "she steals your beauty." I believed she did. I felt so ugly.

A month later, we were newlyweds and still happily married. At least, I thought we were. Some of my friends warned me how blending a family could be challenging at times. Monet felt I let Dean get away with not doing his chores. Dean felt Philip let Monet have her way.

Before we got married, Philip and I knew our kids would try to manipulate or put one against the other. We were determined to stay in love; even when we had issues we couldn't resolve. Eventually, the kids figured out that we were on the same team. They realized they couldn't manipulate or divide us. We were the Steeles.

We had a little spat the other night because he went out with the "boys" and didn't come home until 3:00AM. I didn't know why any married man hung out that late. Especially, since I was in my last trimester. What was he doing out that late every night? I could have gone into labor.

After our spat, he started sleeping in the basement. Every night, I asked him what was wrong. He claimed everything was fine. I knew he was still upset because he stopped coming to bed at night. And he didn't give me my daily massage. Every night, he went to the basement and didn't come upstairs until the next morning.

I walked down to the basement to check on Philip. He heard me coming down the steps.

"What's up Eboni? " he said.

I responded, "I wanted to see what you were doing down here. Are we okay babe?"

He said, "I just needed to catch up on emails from the office."

I was relieved and didn't want him to be upset with me.

Then I asked him, "You need to look at your email this late? Are you coming to bed tonight?"

"Eboni, I'll be upstairs in a minute," he replied.

I walked upstairs and got in the bed. When I dozed off, it was 2 o'clock in the morning. He hadn't made it to bed yet. I kept the light on hoping he would come up before I fell off to sleep.

Around 6:00am the next morning, I rolled over, he still hadn't come to bed. What was he doing downstairs? I looked out the window to see if he left for work. I tiptoed down the steps to the basement. He had fallen asleep on the couch. I called him. "Philip. Are you going to work today, it's 6:00am?"

He jumped up, and walked past me to go upstairs. Moving as fast as I could, I followed him upstairs to the bedroom. "I think I'm going to stay home today; I'm not feeling well. " He didn't seem concerned and proceeded to get ready for work. Dean and Monet had already caught the bus to school.

Before walking out the door to go to work, he walked over and touched my belly, and kissed me on my forehead. Running late for work, he ran out the front door. Something was up. Why was he sleeping in the basement every night? Was he having second thoughts about being married?

Most of my married girlfriends warned me that men do cheat from time to time. One of my girlfriends told me that no marriage was perfect, and it was hard work. My girlfriend Lauren told me that her husband cheated on her the first few years of their marriage. "All men cheat, married or not. Just remember your wedding vows," she said. In so many words, she told me there was a possibility that Philip might have been cheating on me. She told me to focus on keeping my family together.

I peeped out the bedroom window to make sure he pulled out of the driveway. After he drove off, I went to the basement to look around in his office. Pretending I was a detective, I put on my glasses. I snooped around his office. Something was going on and I wanted to get to the bottom of it. It bothered me that he didn't come to bed at night.

Every time I suspected a guy was cheating on me, I was usually right. I trusted my woman's intuition. In the basement, next to the laundry room, Philip had a business phone line. All of a sudden, the business line rang. I answered the phone. "Hello," I said. The person on the other end hung up. I saw the phone number on the caller ID, so I called the number back and hoped the person would pick up.

A woman answered and I said, "Hello. This is Philip Steele's business line.

Can I help you?" The lady on the other end replied, "I must have the wrong phone number. Who are you?"

When I told her I was Philip's wife, she immediately hung up the phone. I wrote down her phone number and continued to scroll through the caller ID. That number was listed on the caller ID, every day and night.

Then I wobbled over to his office to log on his computer. Logging on his computer without his password would be impossible. So, I guessed his password. Men being predictable, I thought his birthdate would be his password. But that didn't work. Then I typed in his social security number. That didn't work. Before I got locked out, I typed in the word "password." Bingo! I got in.

He probably didn't expect anyone would log onto his computer. When I logged in, I remembered the old adage, "if you go looking for something, you will find it." I didn't care because I wanted to know why he was in the basement every night.

Perusing through the folders on the hard drive of his computer, I looked through the Windows temp files to see what websites he had visited. It looked like he had opened several dating sites, downloaded pictures, and sent several emails. I sorted the files by the extension so I could get specific information about each file.

The temp files identified the time and dates he was logged on his computer. Most of the files were logged around midnight up to 2:00am in the morning. I saw that he was in logged at 11:00pm the night before. Looking at the apps on his computer, I saw the ADL icon on his desktop.

ADL was an email application. I couldn't resist logging into his email to see what I would find. He would have been pissed if he knew I was going through his email. As far as I was concerned, when we got married, he didn't have any privacy. We were a team.

I clicked on the ADL icon and it chimed. "You've got mail!" He had 20 email messages from women on the Matchdate.com dating site. My heart started beating fast. I felt myself getting sick. I was devastated. There were over 20 email messages from women. He had been chatting with women from a dating website.

Why was he even on the site? One by one, I opened each message. Ten different women sent email messages to him. I read one email message from Lisa and it read:

"Philip it was nice meeting you. I attached the picture we took at my party. Thanks for celebrating my birthday with me. I will call you tomorrow morning."

After reading her message, I burst into tears. My stomach started hurting. I felt like I was about to go into labor. He was cheating on me with Lisa and other women from dating sites.

If I had the strength, I would have thrown his computer on the floor and trashed his office. Before logging off, I looked through his emails for the picture of Lisa. It looked like he tried to delete it. I sorted through his deleted files on his hard drive and found the image of him and Lisa.

There it was, a picture of them celebrating her birthday. He was dressed up in a suit. She was holding balloons and flowers. Screaming at the top of my lungs. "I CAN'T BELIEVE THIS S _ _ T! Why did he marry me if he wanted to be single?" I printed the image so I could confront him when he got home. He was busted.

I turned off his computer and went back upstairs. Walking up the steps, I called him every name but a child of God. I used a lot of expletives. Finding out that he had been unfaithful to me, hurt so bad. Trying to pull myself together before the kids got home, I took a hot shower, got dressed and watched TV in the family room. I had to calm down so I didn't go into labor.

Monet came in from school and saw that my eyes were puffy and bloodshot red. "What's wrong Ms. Eboni? "she said. I lied and told her that I wasn't feeling well. I kept looking at the clock and couldn't wait for

Philip to get home. He usually got in around 6:00pm, after picking Dean up from football practice.

They walked in right at 6:00pm. Monet was in her room doing homework. When he came over to give me a hug. I pushed him away. "I have a headache." Then I followed him upstairs to the bedroom. As I was walking up the stairs, I was ready to confront him about his infidelity.

"Philip, I need to chat with you, do you have a minute?" Then, he asked, "Have you been crying Eboni?" He noticed my eyes were puffy and red. My first reaction was to slap him in his face, and then present my evidence later. Angrily I replied, "Philip, I've been crying because I discovered that you have been cheating on me." I walked over to the dresser and picked up the picture of him and Lisa posing at her birthday party, and showed it to him.

He sat quiet on the edge of the bed, not saying a word. I handed him the picture. Words could not describe the expression on his face. He was totally busted.

Then he lied. "Eboni, that was a lady I used to date before we met."

"Philip you are a BOLDFACE LIAR! I saw the email message in your mailbox. You were with her the other night celebrating her birthday. I want to know what's going on, RIGHT NOW!", I demanded.

He looked at me in shock. "How did you get into my email Eboni?! Why are you invading my privacy?"

"I can't believe you are on dating sites acting like you are single. We've been married for less than a year and we have a baby on the way. Do you want a DIVORCE Philip?"

"NO. I don't want a divorce Eboni. I'm sorry and promise I won't ever do that again!", he said begging me to forgive him.

"Yes, you are a sorry ass!" I responded.

Philip got off the bed and walked over to hug me as if that would fix what he had done. I wanted to slap him in the face. Looking at him in disgust, I realized I was a fool to marry him. I should have known he was just like most men and he could never be faithful.

He tried to grab me and hold me, but I pushed him away. Following me around the room he kept saying he was sorry. I looked at him in disbelief that he had cheated.

Monet knocked on our bedroom door, "Is everything okay?" Philip walked out of the bedroom and went downstairs.

It took some time to get over his infidelity. I was a new wife with a baby on the way. Philip seemed so perfect. I never thought he'd ever cheat on me. Philip convinced me; that he was different. It wasn't my responsibility to babysit him or try to control his behavior.

I thought about moving out and filing for a divorce. But the Bible said I had to forgive him. I didn't want him to leave me like my father left my mother. I didn't want to bring another baby into the world without a father.

The next morning, Autumn Amber Steele was born on April 10th at 2:10pm at Lincoln Regional Hospital. She weighed 8 lbs. 5 ounces. I cried tears of joy when the doctor said, "It's a girl." I always wanted a daughter. As soon as the nurses cleaned her up and cut the umbilical cord, Philip reached out to hold her in his arms. Looking in her eyes, he got emotional and kissed her little fingers and toes.

The nurse took her from Philip and checked her vitals. They rolled me back to my hospital room. "Within an hour, the nurse brought her to my room in the baby bassinet. Everyone was excited when they rolled her in my room. She was wrapped up in a pink baby blanket. Her eyes were wide open and she was alert.

Dean walked over to Autumn's bassinet. "Let me hold her first Monet." "I want to hold her first," Monet said. She was passed around the room. From Grandma Fran, to Dean, and then Monet. The kids were so excited to hold their baby sister. Passing her around, everyone took turns holding her.

The hospital discharged me and Autumn the next day. Philip picked us up from the hospital. As soon as we got home, Monet and Dean wanted to hold their baby sister. I went upstairs to unpack my bag and change my clothes.

When I walked downstairs to the family room, I noticed Philip had gone downstairs to the basement. Autumn was hungry and started crying so I gave her a bottle. An hour later, Philip was still in the basement.

Philip was downstairs in the basement again. I couldn't think of anything more important than being with his family. The baby and I just got home. I wondered what he was doing in the basement, this time. After I finished burping Autumn, I asked Dean if he could hold her while I went downstairs.

I tiptoed down the steps hoping Philip wouldn't hear me. The television was on but he wasn't watching it. He was in his office. I walked towards his office and heard him on his business phone line. I stood outside of the office to eavesdrop on his conversation.

He was talking low, almost in a whisper. "I just picked up my wife and my daughter from the hospital. I can't talk to you right now. I'll call you tonight. Yes. I still love you." Trying to hold back from screaming on him and busting in his office. I decided to walk away.

I tiptoed back upstairs to the family room with the kids. They were taking turns holding and feeding Autumn. I held back the tears and tried to stay strong. Philip came back upstairs an hour later. I rolled my eyes at him. He didn't know that I heard his telephone conversation with another woman.

The kids and I were sitting in the family room. I didn't let on that I knew what he was doing in the basement. Monet helped me cook dinner. Dean and Philip took turns holding Autumn. When dinner was ready, we ate in the dining room as a family.

I still hadn't healed from Philip's infidelity. It hurt knowing that he hadn't changed and he was still cheating on me. I continued to do my part as his wife. My greatest fear was that Autumn would grow up a fatherless daughter, like me. She deserved to have a father to protect her, love and to be there for her every day.

Both of my children deserved to have a wonderful life, and I was willing to do whatever it took to keep my family together. When I married Philip, it was a leap of faith, hoping to break the cycle of being a single mom and Autumn being a fatherless daughter.

Reflecting on all that had happened in my life, most of my dreams had come true. Even though it took me over 30 years to realize them. I am blessed to have made it through all of my trials and tribulations. I had become a better person and a strong black woman.

At this juncture in my life, I was grateful for everything that God had done in my life. I've continued to work on loving myself more than ever before. I'm a fatherless daughter who came out a winner through it all. Who knows what the future holds for me and my family? But I looked forward to creating new chapters and living a beautiful life.

Sincerely, Mrs. Eboni Steele.

Printed in the United States
By Bookmasters